ANOTHER NOVEL IN THE
(TRANSLAT

April in Portugal
COIMBRA

Marie Warder

Copyright © 2011 Marie Warder
All rights reserved.

ISBN: 1456462393
ISBN-13: 9781456462390

www.dromedarisbooks.com

Box 82 Stn Main, Delta, B.C., V4K 1V0, CANADA
P.O. Box 938, Point Roberts, WA 98281, USA

Library and Archives Canada Cataloguing in Publication

Warder, Marie
April in Portugal / Marie Warder.

(Stories from South Africa)
ISBN 978-0-9733625-4-1

I. Title. II. Series: Warder, Marie. Stories from South Africa.

PS8645.A74A67 2011   C813'.6   C2011-900202-7

Marie Warder
April in Portugal

COIMBRA

In order to claim their share of the estate left by their grandmother, a Portuguese *marquise*, Julieta and Carlos have to be able to prove that they are worthy, and capable of taking their places within the strict, conservative family circle. For this reason the young Carlos, a student in England, and Julieta, who is in her late teens and happens to be living in South Africa at the time, are summoned to Portugal by the Marquis Ricardo da Monsaraz. At the insistence of Julieta's friends, Erin March—who is the secretary to Julieta's lawyer, Cameron Monroe—accompanies the recently bereaved and complex Portuguese girl to Portugal, to keep an eye on her. There, amid the luxurious surroundings of Ricardo da Monsaraz' estate, where one electrifying incident follows another, even the cool, sedate Erin begins to thaw...

Whether it is the unusual setting for this story, the manner in which Marie Warder succeeds in creating suspenseful situations—or whether both elements contribute— there is that touch of 'difference' in this book that elevates it above the level of ordinary recreational reading material.—Louise Behrens, Book Critic SABC

Another novel in the Stories from South Africa series
(Translated from the original Afrikaans)

Acknowledgements:

I am indebted to Luis Wiechers for restoration of the original cover artwork, and, for other assistance, to Keith Bridgefoot, Josephine Cooper, Rowan Reynolds and Shaun Warder—without whose help and encouragement this book could never have been completed.   M.W.

"The most important rule for us is to concentrate on keeping our lives open to God. Let everything else including work, clothes, and food be set aside."

Oswald Chambers: My Utmost For His Highest

Taken from My Utmost for His Highest by Oswald Chambers, © 1935 by Dodd Mead & Co., renewed © 1963 by the Oswald Chambers Publications Assn., Ltd. Used by permission of Discovery House Publishers, Grand Rapids MI 49501. All rights reserved.

OTHER NOVELS BY MARIE WARDER

STORM WATER – ISBN 0-921966-05-9

In exchange for giving him a son, the proud and fascinating Count Louis de Maupassant offers wealth and an elevated position in society.

This historical novel about South Africa, set in the very early days of the Cape of Good Hope, transports the reader to a distant, romantic past – to the adventurous days of the Dutch East India Company, when the Colony was young.

WITH NO REMORSE... – ISBN 0-921966-03-2

An extraordinary narrative of daring and courage, of sacrificial love and rock-solid loyalty is, at the same time, a tale of suspicion and jealousy; of devilish cunning and despicable treachery.

During World War 11, Joshua Naudé, a young South African agronomist, is sent on a clearly defined mission to the strategic island of Malta. His gentle, plucky but frail wife, Anna, accompanies him. Not long after their arrival on the island, they are joined by Joshua's devastatingly good-looking airman brother and, through him, they become acquainted with beautiful and captivating Stephanie Velez; a ruthless charmer of volatile Latin temperament.

Tarnished Idols – 0 921966-07-5

"No mortal is perfect enough to be idolized." Around this proven adage, Marie Warder has woven a gripping tale – a story in which pure love and flaming passion are interchanged with venomous envy and bitter hatred.

In convincing manner, the writer relates the story from the point of view of Paul Jansen, the man who sincerely loves the beautiful Jeanne, but can never be more than a brother to her. The reason? Jeanne already worships another man – an idol with 'feet of clay'. Her initial adoration and later struggle against this 'idol' make for an intensely moving story, sensitively recorded

The Beauclaire Saga #1
Part one of a trilogy.

When you know that you know that you know! – ISBN 0-921966-09-1
or
The redemption of Benjamin Ashton

Under the Southern Cross, an awesome awakening amid the orange blossom on a South African Citrus Farm.

Set amid orange groves in the lovely town of Nelspruit, South Africa—among 'Bougainvilleas, Flame trees, Jacarandas and Poinsettias; Scarlet Flamboyant and Bottle Brush, yellow Bird of Paradise, crimson Erythrina, salmon, rose pink and white Oleander, interspersed by a riot of the sky blue, Duranta'—the air is heavy with the perfume of orange blossom in this well-written novel with an unusual plot, unusual complications and an unusual conclusion. It is the story of a successful young American, one of the wealthiest men in the world, who travels to South Africa where, going in search of his brother, he finds God—and, in so doing, finds himself! To say more would be to spoil for our readers what should prove to be a captivating read.

THE BEAUCLAIRE SAGA #2

DOMINIC VERWEY: SAMARITAN OF THE SAHARA

In the stockade of an outlaw band in the Sahara desert, Doctor Dominic Verwey is introduced to the Bedouin chief as '**Sahbena el-Hakim**' — my friend, the doctor. But he would very shortly thereafter earn a second name; that of '**Hamid Pasha**' — protector and leader of his people, 'refuge of the refugee and sanctuary of the oppressed'. His main purpose is to settle a score with the unprincipled Arab, Abdel Sharia, who incarcerates innocent men in his labour camps and enslaves beautiful women in his harem…

THE BEAUCLAIRE SAGA #3

THE YARDSTICK – ISBN: 978-0-9733625

'*The Yardstick*' was this author's 22nd novel, Volume three of the gripping Beauclaire Saga, and her seventh book to be written in Canada. Although so much of the story is played out among the dunes of the *Kalahari Desert* of the Northern Cape Province of South Africa, we are also taken back to Nelspruit, Johannesburg and Louisiana, and recognize some

Marie Warder

of the well-loved characters from *When you know that you know that you know*, as the Beauclaire saga continues. *(Dedication: In loving memory of Tom... One cannot measure anything without some scale of measurement, whether it be visible, tangible, audible, or even experiential. One needs a yardstick — and you remain mine!)*

NON-FICTION

The Bronze Killer:New Edition – ISBN 0968735800

'Original Edition ... Autographed Collectors' Item - ISBN 0889258856
The Bronze Killer: New Edition — Dromedaris Books

The story of a family's fight against Hemochromatosis – the most common Genetic disorder – including the first-ever 'layman's' reference: "Iron ... the other side of the story!"

THE BOOK THAT GAVE A DISEASE A NEW NAME, *evolved from 'Iron...the other side of the story!' (1984) which was the first book ever to be devoted entirely to the subject of Hemochromatosis — iron overload. (Please note alternative spelling, outside of North America, where the disorder is known as 'Haemochromatosis'.)*

Since this book was first published in 1989, thousands of families around the world have found it to be a valuable resource. More than just the personal account of a family who have suffered through the ravages of this terrible disease, it has been a source of information, encouragement and enlightenment to many. Included is *'IRON ... the other side of the story!'* which provided the world with the first 'layperson's reference to the genetic disorder that, if untreated, can lead to a destructive overload of iron in the body; far too often with fatal results. Recommended by physicians and clinics in Canada and further afield, *'The Bronze Killer'* earned high praise for the author in her 1991 citation for the Canada

Volunteer Medal of Honour and Certificate of Honour, which read in part: *"Through Marie's research and most noted book, 'The Bronze Killer', she has educated doctors and the general public about the disease. As a result, Hemochromatosis is now recognized as Canada's most common genetic disorder and routine blood tests for the disease may soon become standard diagnostic procedure."*

Hemochromatosis. — There was a time when nine out of ten people had never heard of it, and physicians considered it to be 'too rare to be of concern'. It is now known to be the most common genetic disorder of all, and Marie Warder has played no small part in, as she puts is 'bringing the research that was mouldering on the shelves or in the filing cabinets, into the light of day'. In *The Bronze Killer,* she provides much needed information about this common enemy, from recognizing its symptoms to stressing the importance of early detection and treatment.

The Dromedaris Concept

Dromedary: *Camelus Dromedarius*: a one-humped camel. Camels are commonly regarded as carriers – of both people and merchandise. ***Dromedaris*** was also the name of a ship which took our ancestors to South Africa in 1652. Our mandate, in the 'Dromedaris concept', is to bring a different kind of merchandise from South Africa to the rest of the world. … Our books, written by acclaimed expatriate authors.

About the Author

Before immigrating to Canada, Marie Warder was listed among South Africa's top seven "favourite novelists" by a South African Book Club. She was certainly one of the most prolific. Mary Morrison Webster, book critic of the prestigious Sunday Times, once recorded among her recommendations, two books written "in time for Christmas—in two different languages." Mrs. Warder's biography is included in the Archives of the National Council of Women among "Notable Women of Johannesburg."

Locally, where the lives in British Columbia, she was familiar for many years as a chaplain at the Delta Hospital while, to most people in the rest of the world, she is known chiefly as the Founder and President Emeritus of both the Canadian and South African Hemochromatosis Societies, and the Founder and former President of the International Association of Haemochromatosis Societies. Few know that, before embarking on her two ground-breaking books on Hemochromatosis made available, together, in 2000, in the 'new edition' of *The Bronze Killer*, the 'internationally acclaimed best-seller' (Delta Optimist), which contributed to her being awarded a medal of honour and certificate of honour in Canada—she was already the author of 16 very successful novels; three of them used in South African schools. Not surprisingly, many of her stories take place in and around newspaper offices for, according to 'The Journalist', she became, at the age of seventeen, the youngest chief reporter in the world, having sold her first newspaper article at the age of 11 and her first short story at 17. During her career as a journalist she interviewed some the world's most famous people.

All in all, it seemed that she had a good career ahead of her in her native South Africa, but when—just before her 17th birthday—Frederick Abinger (Tom) Warder, a handsome, tanned young man in an Air Force uniform walked into the newspaper office one day, her life changed radically. It was a clear case of 'love at first sight' and, after that meeting, her life would revolve about him. She played the piano in Tom's very popular dance band; he was wholeheartedly supportive of her writing. And whenever there was a sword fight to be fought in a novel, or a chess game to be played, it would be her husband who worked out the moves for her.

When he was 42, he suddenly became ill and, as she tells in the book, ***The Bronze Killer,*** they had come to the end of the good times. For more than 28 years after that, except for a series of travel articles for a magazine she devoted her literary efforts entirely to the writing of more than 200 articles on the subject of Hemochromatosis, and to the production of patient literature for individuals, hospitals and other medical facilities. Her newsletters and brochures have gone out to more than 16 countries. Now she believes that she has done all in her power to promote awareness of the world's most common genetic disorder. Late in 2003, motivated by the discovery of the tattered scraps of the only carbon copy of the long-lost manuscript of a book, she decided that she was ready to move on. ***Storm Water*** and ***With no remorse...*** were released simultaneously less than a year later.

When you know that you know that you know! or The redemption of Benjamin Ashton (April 2005) caused a sensation. The response has been phenomenal. One reader describes it as "The best novel I have ever read!" Another reports that she read it "four times in less than a month", and wished that it were "twice as long!" This about a book that contains 576 pages! The setting of that book is a citrus farm called '*Beauclaire*', situated in the district of Nelspruit in South Africa, and, responding to the clamour for more about Benjamin (Ash) Ashton and his friends, 'Dominic Verwey: Samaritan of the Sahara' — although of a different genre — continued the 'Beauclaire saga' in 2006.

About this book one reviewer wrote, "After the success of her South African novel, ***Tarnished Idols,*** Marie Warder has gone to the other end of Africa for the setting of her new one, ***Samaritan of the Sahara.*** Mrs. Warder's romantic imagination and facile pen provide plenty of local colour, and she captures the reader's attention from start to finish. The very unusual theme concerns the adventures of a doctor in the Sahara who, besides being skilled with the scalpel, is also a dashing figure of the Robin Hood type. Well worth reading and highly recommended."

Released on July 9/2007, **'The Yardstick'** was this author's 21st book, ***Volume three*** of the gripping ***Beauclaire Saga,*** her seventh book to be written in Canada. Although so much of the story is played out among the dunes of the Kalahari Desert of the Northern Cape Province of South Africa, we are also taken back to Nelspruit and Johannesburg, and recognize some of the well-loved characters from ***When you know that you know that you know,*** as the Beauclaire saga continues. We find a disillusioned Benjamin Ashton —

about to become a grandfather, forced to consider relocating the South African members of his family, which could well bring to an end what has been for them a blessedly happy era in the enthralling *Beauclaire* saga. At the same time, the integrity of Ben's altruistic son, a physician, is severely tested as Jordan is unwillingly drawn into the sordid affairs of Tristan Connaught, the womanizing partner in their upscale practice near Johannesburg.

Unfortunately Tristan is none other than the son of Father Clifford Connaught of Bethlehem in the Free State, who played such a important role in the lives of both Ben Ashton and his brother, Jamie; and, together with them, we are re-introduced to many of the other well-loved characters from **'When you know that you know that you know! or The redemption of Benjamin Ashton.'   Publisher**

PENNY OF THE MORNING STAR — RELEASED IN DECEMBER 2010

"Penny of the Morning Star," was commissioned more than fifty years ago for use by ESL students in South African schools. At that time it contained an English/Afrikaans glossary and comprehension questions, but even then students would rather discuss the characters—particularly why, in his early thirties, the *Morning Star* editor Paul Jansen was prematurely grey and his behaviour often so unpredictable. The author admits that she could not really explain those characteristics, even to herself, which is why she felt so strongly that what would now very likely have to be the last book she would ever publish, would have to be a *re-write* of *Penny*—not as a school book this time—and completely updated, while still set in the post-war 1940's ... because, having witnessed what happened to some of those very students after the Angolan War, she is finally able to able to understand that editor!

A book for all ages. Delightful! Refreshing! Highly Recommended!

—Elaine Murray

Recommended reading age: **Unlimited!**
—Michelle Rankin

Having followed this writer's career for many years before she embarked on the successful Dromedaris "Stories from South Africa" series, I can truthfully say that I have never been disappointed. I have found that even a story like this, clearly written for people much younger than I am now, still held my attention from start to finish. I am pleased to award it five stars!

—Richard Seymour

This charming story will certainly inspire young people who have ambitions to write, to follow their dreams.

—Josie Cooper

April in Portugal
COIMBRA

Chapter One

As the years have gone by, it has been tragic to see pictures of people in Mozambique with limbs blown off by landmines—a situation later brought to the attention of the world by people like Princess Diana—and to learn of the desperate state of affairs in a neighboring country; but somehow I had not connected the revolution with what later happened in Angola. In fact, until then, I had never given any of it very much thought at all! What had made everything so confusing at the time, to most South Africans as young as I was then, was that there were so many rebel 'factions' (for want of a better description) all referred to only by letters of the alphabet, that eventually I could not remember which was which. I certainly could not do so at that time, and not even later, as I sat there that day so long ago, listening raptly way back in 1956, to Cameron Monroe, my employer, relate Julieta's intriguing story.

"Isn't the liberation movement in Mozambique called FRELIMO? Short for "Free Mozambique, or something?" I was obliged to ask, risking the revelation of my ignorance while moved to exhibit some degree of interest.

"That's correct. And, apart from FRELIMO in Mozambique, and ZANLA and ZIPRA in Zimbabwe, there are the liberation movements of SWAPO in Namibia, the MPLA in Angola, and the ANC and PAC in South Africa. All are reported to be supported by the Marxist Eastern Block, and they're all fighting to get rid of the colonial yoke in the subcontinent."

I was too ashamed to confess to the lawyer for whom I had worked for many years, that, as rumors about the South African involvement spreading from Angola to the border of South-West Africa were confirmed, I had tried very hard not to worry too much about a situation which, for me, remained remote, and I found difficulty in revealing that before I had met Julieta da Monsaraz, and until the coup in Lourenço[1] Marques had begun to send vast numbers of people across our borders as refugees from Mozambique, I, the competent, self-assured Erin March had been under a total misapprehension about other facts as well.

Although, according to my school history books, the Portuguese had been the first Europeans to set foot on South African soil, and as far back as the early fifteenth century, the only Portuguese people I had personally encountered in the parts of Johannesburg that I frequented, were the friendly, rather burly owners of my local greengrocer shop. Consequently, on the day she was introduced to me as my factotum or 'gopher', the vivacious, refined, well-educated young girl with the mischievous little face and halo of shining, ebony-black curls, was a complete surprise. Fortunately Mr. Monroe seemed amused when, with some embarrassment, I steeled myself to tell him that!

"Oh gosh, no!" he laughed. "Then you know only a minute section of the Portuguese community. There are some, particularly in the Azores, Madeira and places like that—mostly the islanders—who become, as you say, excellent market gar-

---

[1] Now Lorenzo

deners and greengrocers; but, ask Julieta…they hardly speak the same language. And if you've never been to a Portuguese restaurant, you have really missed out!"

I smiled apologetically. However, before I could get another word in, he drew a chair closer to my desk, sat down back-to-front upon it, and, crossing his arms, leant confidingly across the back of it. I prepared myself. … My boss was winding up to it and would, at any moment, launch into one of his favorite topics of conversation. … I fully expected him to begin with: "When I went on my first trip around the world …"

With a sigh of resignation, I set my pen down and forced my wintry smile to become a tad more indulgent. I was sure I had guessed right. I knew him so well. … It transpired, however, that this time, there was to be a different slant to the account.

"I had already been friendly with Julieta's parents for some years before that," he told me, "but that is when, with their intervention, I came to know members of her extended family overseas.—Do you know that Portugal is one of the few places where one still bumps into real princes and princesses on a regular basis? If you want to see some wonderful old mansions and estates, encounter rare and noble courtesy and some of the most valuable antiques, family silver and priceless works of art, as well as examples of the most exquisite old lace in the world, you only have to journey through Portugal?"

It was a stifling summer afternoon in December, airless and enervating as only a Monday in the Golden City could be, and, ever-conscious of my cluttered desk, veritably groaning under the piles of uncompleted work which had to be finished before the Christmas holidays, I closed my eyes insensitively to the undisguised enthusiasm which lit up his attractive face, and brutally tried to head him off before too much more of my precious afternoon was wasted.

"She appears to be a perky little soul," I observed dryly, and gestured in the direction of where, in the office adjoining mine, Julieta was sorting documents for filing. My workstation was situated diagonally across from the door, so that, from where we were sitting, only her back and bowed shoulders were visible to us. "As long as she is not afraid of hard work, the two of us will get on well together. But," it suddenly occurred to me to ask, "what is she doing here in Johannesburg? Are her parents also here?"

"Both died within a short time of one another in LM[2] last year, soon after the first shots in the revolution were fired, and Julieta now has no relatives in Africa. She is staying temporarily in Dunkeld, with an old family friend, until matters can be arranged for her to return to Portugal…"

"The poor child. She must sometimes feel quite lost here among strangers. But when you say 'temporarily' does that mean that she will only be working here in the office on a temporary basis?"

The very thought was disturbing to me. The work and routine in a legal office differ so radically from what is required in any other, that the training of yet another employee would necessarily cost me a great deal of overtime and effort—not to mention patience! I really did not want to invest time and energy in Julieta da Monsaraz if I had to go through it all again with someone else in a few weeks, or even months. The simple prospect of it made me sigh all over again.

"Oh, don't let that upset you." He smiled sympathetically, as though he could read my thoughts.—That sigh must have spoken volumes!—"Perhaps 'temporarily' wasn't the right word. What I really meant to say was that her stay here is indeterminate." He continued to look at me in a kindly

---

[2] (Lourenco Marques)

manner, but there was that pleading note in that beautifully moderated voice which, I can tell you, had swayed many a jury!

"It's an interesting, but long story, and I know that you are very busy, Erin," he went on to say. "However I think I must tell it to you because, once you understand, you will find it easier to be more tolerant of her, I'm sure.—And, the Lord only knows, she could do with a bit of kindness!"

The reference to how busy I was immediately made me feel guilty. Cameron Monroe, or "C.M' as the staff referred to him, was the ideal employer. He was undoubtedly the most patient, understanding man alive, and when I had first begun to work for him he had certainly needed more than *his* fair share of patience! Nearly ten years earlier, when I had first taken my place at the very desk which had now been allocated to Julieta, he had personally seen to it that every obstacle was smoothly overcome, and many of my foolish mistakes were either overlooked or tactfully swept aside. Whenever the woman who was then his personal and private secretary reached the stage where she was ready to give up on me—as I would probably be driven to do with Julieta da Monzaraz, in the very near future—he had unfailingly intervened on my behalf, pleading my youth and inexperience in my defense. "It cannot be expected of Miss March to know what she has not yet learned," he would remonstrate gently.

It occurred to me that perhaps it was for that very reason that I had, of late, begun to take as much work as possible off his shoulders. He was trying valiantly to quit smoking at that time, and I studied him closely as he lit a cigarette, exhaled the first puff, and then determinedly stubbed it out. To my mind, it would have been criminal to saddle him with the thousand-and-one small matters that I was now quite capable of handling, myself. He had more than enough to deal with, as it was, and his fatigue was clearly discernible to anyone who knew him as well as I did.

I suddenly realized, to my surprise, that the past ten years had changed him, and something began to niggle at my conscience. As he sat there before me in the harsh summer light, he was still every bit the same, capable attorney he had always been; good-looking—even more so, if the truth were told—faultlessly clad in a well-tailored suit, wearing a fashionable silk tie with matching handkerchief in his top pocket. But the lines around his eyes were more deeply etched and I detected a minute touch of grey just beginning to show at his temples.

"Can it be possible?" I asked myself, "that he can be heading towards thirty-five?" Then it hit me: "And, good heavens, I'll soon be twenty-eight, myself!"

As if he could feel my eyes upon him, he looked up, almost startled, and smiled; his teeth still perfect and sparkling white in his tanned face. While I was thinking how nice it was that his eyes almost crinkled shut when he smiled, he tried sheepishly to rub away the ash—which he had accidentally allowed to fall, into the carpet—with the toe of his shoe. Then, without a vestige of doubt, I knew what was niggling at me.

What was the world coming to when a man was too terrified to drop as much as a spot of ash on his own floor, in his own office! ... When his secretary had the audacity to hint that she had too much work, and was too to busy to be able to listen to him when he wished to talk! To indicate by her attitude that her employer was wasting her time and bored her, when he felt like relaxing for a moment! My blood ran cold as I realized that, for years, I had probably been striving, albeit unconsciously, to reach precisely the stage where it was more my office than his! My rationalizing of a few minutes before had been pure hypocrisy. A false excuse to justify my ambition. 'Erin March, the competent; the indispensable—the disciplinarian!' *The tyrant!'* my conscience mocked me. Cameron paid me enough, in both money and respect, to expect that I should at least be prepared to listen, no matter what he had to say!

Considerably chastened by what I had just discovered about myself, I looked directly at him and gave my full attention to what he had to tell about Julieta.

"I don't really have as much work as I might pretend," I admitted, with a forced half-laugh. "That's purely an attitude I adopt to keep you convinced that I am worth my salary. Please tell me. ... I should very much like to hear the story."

It was an interesting tale. I was astonished to learn, among other details, that someday—when she was twenty-one—Julieta stood to inherit a significant fortune. "But it's not all as simple as it sounds," Cameron Monroe added. "In order to grasp all the ramifications of the situation you would need to know more about Julieta's grandmother. You would have needed to know that lady very well indeed, when she was alive, before you could even *begin* to understand either her, or her actions.

"The *marquise* was a regular old tyrant—perhaps 'martinet' would more suitably describe her—and she ruled both her family and her servants with a rod of iron. Try to picture her, as she was when I saw her for the first time: a sprightly, upright, elegant old dame, in that veritable castle of a house—known locally as her *palácio.* Wizened by age but fiercely independent, she was absolutely unbending in her attitude towards those around her. She asked nothing of anyone else ... ever mindful of the endless procession of Da Monsaraz feet which had trod those massive, tiled halls, before her, and relentless in her efforts to control the footsteps of those who would follow.

"She possessed vast estates—she must have been extremely wealthy—and she treated the peasants who worked her lands as if she were an empress and they her subjects. ... The Portuguese monarchy was abolished on October 5th in 1910, when King Manuel II was deposed following a republican revolution, but as far as she, her family and her underlings were concerned, that had never happened. Members of that family continued to consider themselves to be of the aristocracy."

"Can there still be such people in the world?...Such a state of affairs?" escaped me almost involuntarily.

"Certainly...it was so when I was there many years ago—and in a moment I'll tell you about another who most definitely remains one to this day! Furthermore, her tenants and employees more or less expected that of their *marquise*. Under such an almost feudal system the farmers would have been—and probably still are—disappointed in any member of what they consider as the nobility who is in any way familiar with them. They need to have someone they respect and can look up to."

I nodded in understanding, by this time completed fascinated by what sounded to me like at tale from the Middle Ages.

"I can't say that I particularly liked her too much—her children could surely not have *loved* her—but I felt a reluctant admiration for her. She had that gift of eliciting both admiration and awe. Before her thirtieth birthday she had already given birth to seven children, but managed to raise only four of them—three sons and a daughter. I met two of those sons when I was there on holiday.

"Ricardo, the eldest, had died the previous year, but I was able to meet his son...another Ricardo, who was then about seventeen. He lived with his grandmother and he struck me as an extraordinary person because he so obviously adored the old lady. ... Probably one of the few people in the world who cherished for her any sentiment besides fear.

"I also learnt to know Carlos, the second eldest, because he happened to be in Portugal at the time, but it was Mario, the youngest, who was actually my friend. He was Julieta's father, and it was through him that I became acquainted with all the others.

"And the sister?" I wanted to know." Is she still alive?"

"Luisa? ... Oh, yes—there's no doubt about her! She, her husband and family lived on a wine farm in the south, quite a distance from the *palácio* and, for some reason or another, we never bumped into one another. She fitted in somewhere between the youngest, and Carlos. Her oldest child must be somewhat older than Julieta, who could not have been more that about two at that time. That was more than seventeen years ago, remember!"

He broke off for a moment to take another cigarette, did not light it, however, and replaced it in his silver cigarette case. "I *have* to give this up," he muttered wryly. "Filthy habit!"

I said nothing, waiting impatiently for him to pick up the story once more.

"Among the Portuguese 'nobility'," he resumed at last, "a marriage tends to be more like a state treaty than anything else.—Now you shall see where Julieta fits into the saga.

"Two of the *marquise's* children obliged her by taking marriage partners of her choice. Ricardo, the eldest, married a cousin, a fabulously wealthy young lady with a few hectares under olive trees in the country, and several properties on the islands, which doubtless made her even more desirable in the old girl's eyes. The grandson, Ricardo—to whom I have already referred—is thus the present marquis and, as such, is the head of the family.

"The bridegroom for Luisa, the only daughter, was chosen, and virtually 'reserved' for her when she was still in rompers, and even she bowed to the will of her mother, but the other two ..." He shrugged, shaking his head eloquently as he did so. "During a visit to England, Carlos , the second eldest, fell in love, with a young Scottish girl who was performing in some musical show or other, and Manuel, the youngest, accepted a government job in Lourenco Marques, where, within six months of his arrival, he married Julieta's mother. She was a teacher in South Africa, in the Orange Free State, and was vacationing in LM where she met Manuel."

"So she was a South African?" I asked, surprised.

"My dear girl, she was an Afrikaner! She and Angela Meiring, with whom Julieta is now staying, had shared a school bench in Bethal."

For quite a few moments I found myself studying what I could see of Julieta's dark, shoulder-length curls through the slightly open door, where she sat with her back to us, and pondering the significance of all that the attorney had just told me. "That must have been a slap in the face for her 'Excellency,'" I finally observed. "Not satisfied to disregard her wishes, they had to make matters worse by choosing women from other countries—or so it must have seemed to her!"

"Precisely. Her immediate reaction was to disown both of them immediately. Later she softened to the extent that she invited them to bring their families home, where she was prepared to welcome them cordially and 'inspect' them.—I tell you, Erin, I pitied those daughters-in-law of hers! Once I came to know the family well, I advised Mario to take his wife and child back to Lourenco Marques, for there Julieta would at least be closer to people who could understand her, and where he, himself, had quite a few acquaintances..."

"But Julieta?" I interrupted him.

"I'm coming to her. All the things I've just been telling you, are of course old history now. The old lady died two years ago, Luisa's children are all grown up—in fact I have an idea that she's already a grandmother—'young' Ricardo must be quite a man of the world by this time—all the Da Monsaraz properties are his now—and here is little Julieta, already a young lady, and one of my employees to boot!

"Only when the old *marquise's* will was read, were the rest of the family reminded of the existence of Carlos and Manuel's children. She may well have done as she threatened, and disowned her two sons, but she remembered her grandchildren. In my opinion this is going to be a very difficult will to probate, and I certainly don't envy Ricardo his situation!"

"What does he have to do with this?"

"A great deal. As the present head of the family, he is the executor as well as the principal heir. In terms of the marquise's will he also has to decide how much money is due to Julieta and the others.—That's the kind of twisted sense of humour that she had! It speaks for itself that provision has been made for Luisa's children, out of the Da Monsaraz property, but the old lady has left her own, personal fortune to the children of Mario and Carlos, on condition that they wait until Julieta, the youngest grandchild, comes of age—probably so that she will then be in a better position to protect her own interests. There are certain other particulars that have to be taken into consideration; most important among them that Julieta and her cousin—both descendents of the 'lost' members on the family—would first have to prove that they are perfectly qualified, in every respect, and capable of taking their places within the family circle. For Julieta, the child of such parents, it's going to be more difficult than she can ever even *begin* to imagine!"

While I sat listening so impersonally to a very complicated drama in which pure strangers were involved, I could of course not have had any premonition of how the trials, tribulations—and private affairs—of my new young office assistant would affect my own future! At that stage I could not for the life of me understand why the girl should necessarily be in for such a particularly hard time. ... That 'Ricardo' relative of hers was, after all, a product of the 20th century, and, in my opinion, did not necessarily need to be as difficult as his arrogant and autocratic grandmother must have been.

It did not take long for me to get to know Julieta very well indeed, but it was not quite so easy to understand her. She was a singular mixture of maturity, naiveté, and childishness. In addition, like many fascinating girls of her race, she had been strictly-raised, but that in no way detracted from the fact that she was also a born coquette! Perhaps it was the ridiculously high heels of the brightly-coloured shoes she invariably wore, which necessarily drew attention to her incredibly small feet, and were the reason why she simply could not walk without swaying her hips provocatively. Her full, scarlet lips were a facial feature which could easily betray her thoughts, however, because, like a child, she could very quickly exchange a smile for a pout if things did not go precisely as she wanted them to. That irritated me at first, but, for some reason or another, she soon made it more than clear that she had placed me on a pedestal, and it was consequently difficult for me not to like her. Who does not weaken in the face of genuine admiration?

Sometimes, when I recalled our conversation at the time when he first told me about her, Cameron's use of the word 'kind,' made me smile cynically. I knew too well that the other females in the office regarded me as something of a dragon. I also knew that some of them were of the opinion that I was, metaphorically speaking, 'on the shelf!'

Upon first suspecting that, I was truly upset. When I arrived home after office-hours that day, I rushed to the mirror and studied my face closely. It was with boundless relief that I could ascertain that it was still both smooth and wrinkle-free under the sharp light above my dressing table. Then frantically snatching the stylish little hat—an eloquent symbol of my elevated financial situation—from my head, I was also grateful to find that there was not a single grey hair to be seen. I comforted myself, before I went to bed, with the thought that, in any case, it was such a pale blonde color that one would have to search very diligently in order to be able to discern grey hairs among the rest—even if there were some; but, for the first time since I'd come to live there, the spacious rooms of my luxurious apartment, and the elegant furniture and carpets which I had collected so joyously, no longer provided me with the same degree of fulfillment.

It was not as if I had never had any opportunities. In the past I had rejected quite a few proposals of marriage. It was just that I had never fallen for any man for whom I would happily give up my career.—But still, things like this were food for thought, and then, to add to my troubled state of mind, when my employer was telling me about Julieta, I had been reminded again of how the years were flying by! It would take many years before I would realize how 'dead' I had been ever since my parents were burned to death by intruders on our farm. In shutting out that memory, I had simultaneously banished all sentiment and deep emotion from my subconscious,

Perhaps it was because Cameron Monroe had requested me to do so that I took the Portuguese girl under my wing. More probably, it was because her genuine admiration was such balm for my wounded ego. I only know that Julieta always made me feel stylish, self-assured and attractive. Because she, herself, was so dark, my blonde hair and blue eyes evidently proved to be an endless source of admiration for her, and—probably to the great amusement of the other girls in the office—she openly declared her affection for her 'dear *Señorita* Erin!' Even our employer eventually observed that I appeared to have acquired a 'willing slave!'

Whatever my reasons for encouraging the girl might have been in the early days, I finally learned to like her, sincerely. It was impossible not to be attached to her since she was as lovable as an impish small kitten, and just as harmless. Furthermore I pitied her for her loneliness in this strange city and consequently began to take her about with me as much as possible.

She could not get over it that I, like the other women on our staff, enjoyed such freedom of movement. In the beginning she found the fact that we could go out at night without a chaperone, almost unbelievable. She was clearly flabbergasted when Suzanne Tredoux complained that her grandfather had forbidden her to play tennis, in shorts, with a male friend, until Julieta heard her talking about that one-day. "You find *that* infuriating *Señorita* Tredoux?" she asked, genuinely astounded. "After the grandfather has kindly permitted you, ***yourself***, to make the arrangement with the young man with whom you are going to play?"

She clearly found our ingratitude shocking! *Bondade divina*! Some of her mother's friends in Lorenzo Marques had to get a letter of permission from their spouses before they could as much as go on holiday, and then they also had to be sure to have another ensuring that they were entitled to return!

"*Never*! I simply don't believe that!" Suzanne said incredulously.

"But it is the absolute truth," Julieta assured her earnestly.[3] "One woman I know, personally, went to visit her parents in Lisbon, and, in her absence, her spouse found a substitute who very soon replaced the absent wife in his affections. He consequently failed to provide his legal wife with the necessary paperwork, and made it known in no uncertain terms that she should remain with her parents; but the rejected lady in question possessed a stronger will than he suspected. Without hesitation, she embarked on the first available ship and sailed back to LM.

"Of course the authorities would not permit her to land without the necessary documentation," I could hear her telling the other women in all earnest, "but fortunately while she was cooling her heels on board, her husband discovered that the other female had packed her belongings that very morning, and had disappeared without trace. He then very promptly went and released his wife—just in time! The ship was already on the point of returning to Lisbon!"

A buzz of conversation ensued, and then Suzanne remarked dryly, "What does the old proverb say...? 'Half a loaf is better than none!'" She laughed so uproariously at her own wit, that it was impossible for me to hear the rest of what followed very clearly; however, the episode was food for some very deep reflection.

Although I generally remained in my own office, it was seldom difficult for me to hear what was going on next door, and this was not the first nor the last conversation in which Julieta expressed her longing for a less restricted way of life; nor was this the first time she had sounded openly envious of

---

[3] Please note: The 'story' content of this book is entirely fictional, but a girl called Julieta did indeed exist, and it is to her that I owe this anecdote.

the others, but I found myself pondering the far-fetched incident she related that afternoon, more deeply.

Whether the story was true or not, I began, for the first time, to understand fully what Monroe had meant when he said, "It is going to be more difficult for Julieta, the child of such parents, than she can ever imagine!"

It was on the following morning that I received a phone call from Mrs. Angela Meiring—the old school friend of Julieta's mother, with whom she, Julieta was staying. Naturally I was surprised when the reputedly very busy 'socialite' invited me to dinner! I could not help wondering how she could find the time to keep an evening open for me.

Like most dwellers in the Golden City, I was familiar with the name, Angela Meiring. As one of Johannesburg's leading hostesses as well as probably the most charming among the comparatively younger members of 'high society,' her photograph was frequently featured in the leading newspapers, and when I had parked my matchbox of a car in front of her imposing Dunkeld mansion, I walked towards the front door conscious of mingled curiosity and nervousness. I need not have been concerned! She proved to be one of the nicest, most unassuming people it had ever been my privilege to meet.— And, my goodness, could she talk!

Her hair was turning grey, but if I closed my eyes it would have been easy to imagine that that musical voice and infectious laugh belonged to a schoolgirl. All the time she was speaking I was aware of a suppressed sense of fun which could bubble over at the slightest provocation. Outwardly, for Angela Meiring, life was just one, long wonderful adventure, but she could also become really serious—as I would later find out when we began to talk about Julieta.

She opened the front door herself. And the moment I looked up into the twinkling brown eyes, I at once felt at home.

"So this is the famous Erin March?!" she said, in welcoming me. "The paragon of all that is perfect. Come...take off your hat and your jacket, so that I can have a better look at this...this shining example of superlative wisdom! The epitome of all charm!

"I was almost afraid to open the door to you," she admitted, seeming to mean it. "After all that Julieta has told me about you, I have imagined an awe-inspiring person ... a sort of mixture between Marilyn Monroe and a Sunday- school teacher, if such a being were humanly possible!"

She appeared to be the only member of the household at home, and the questions I longed to ask must have been easily discernible on my face, because my hostess suddenly smiled and confessed: "I gave my husband instructions to take Julieta and my sister's daughter to a movie so that the two of us could be alone and talk unhindered."

Later, when we were seated at the magnificent Stinkwood[4] table in the dining room, she surprised me again by observing: "And now you're probably sitting there wondering when I'm going to explain why I invited you to come and have dinner with me, not so? Have I guessed correctly?"

Of course I had to admit, with an embarrassed smile, that that was precisely what is was going through my mind at that moment.

"Well then, I'll tell you." She regarded me almost mischievously. "In the first place I was dying of curiosity to see

---

[4] 'Satiny' wood of the precious, *Stinkwood* tree, *Ocotea bullata*, which is found in other rainforests of South Africa, but is known to grows best in the Knysna forest of the Cape Province.

what you look like. You know of course Julieta absolutely idolizes you?—And, secondly, I wanted to satisfy myself that you were a suitable person to be permitted to have so much influence over her!"

In spite of myself I had to smile. Her frankness was overwhelming and yet in no way insulting. When I looked up, it was clear that no malice lurked behind her words, and, to my own amazement, I was not able to take offense.

"And now?" I asked dryly, determined that, if we were going to be so open with one another, I would meet her more than half way. "Now what is the verdict?"

Suddenly I found myself wanting very much for it to be a favorable one.

This time it was she who should have been discomfited, but no! In no way put out, she suddenly became very serious and set her knife and fork down on her plate. She narrowed her eyes as if she were acutely examining my every feature. "Look Erin," she asked earnestly, "do you have any idea of the immense responsibility that now rests on your shoulders? ... I doubt it—but, just to give you some idea of how the situation has disturbed me, I can tell you honestly that, for the past three months I have slept very badly. You can't blame me if I'm being too careful. My peace of mind depends on it!"

I could think of no comment and she continued...

"You have given me a pleasant surprise. ... No, don't look so uncomfortable! Let's just be completely honest with one another. You are older than I expected and you strike me as a well-educated and uncommonly understanding, person." Unexpectedly her suppressed sense of humor succeeded in bubbling over again, and the sparkle in her dark eyes immediately betrayed this. "My dear, the more ladylike Julieta's friends are, the better that suits me! ... Do you have any idea of her circumstances?"

"Mr. Monroe did tell me the story on the day she started work with us."

"In that case I don't have to say much more than that, except that I was aware that you had begun to take her about with you quite a lot lately and I was worried about it."

"But why?" I could not have sounded any more surprised than I felt. "I would've thought that you would appreciate that; particularly because it must be difficult, at times, to keep her entertained. I remember only too well how easy it was to be bored at that age."

"That may be true, but Julieta's situation is different." She moved the crystal jug closer to me, and, indicating that I should help myself to some of the cream to have with the enormous piece of apple pie which she had just placed on my plate, she went on: "I am so afraid ... so terribly afraid that she will become too fond of this kind of life in which she now enjoys complete freedom. We—my husband and I—find it well-nigh impossible, as it is, to restrict her comings and goings. We are not used to exhibiting such narrow-mindedness! What would you have done...?" she asked with one eyebrow raised questioningly, "if you had had parents that refused to let you even go out on the street by yourself? Always insisting that one of them had to company you if you went to a dance or to the theatre? Good gracious I would've been an old maid if Casper had had to put up with that sort of nonsense!"

With that such a comical expression crossed her expressive face that I had to laugh. She then also began to giggle, and suddenly we were both doubled up with mirth, as only two females who have much in common are able to do.

"Oh, dear me, I wonder how any of the young swains who came to fetch me to go dancing in my young days would have reacted if my mother, resplendent a tight satin, 'cross-cut' evening gown and the sharp-pointed dancing shoes of the period, had chosen to make a sudden appearance and announced that she was accompanying us!"

"But, in any case, from what you tell me, and using Julieta's situation as a parallel, he would probably not have been permitted to fetch you, in the first place," I reminded her when I could speak coherently at last. "Julieta's admirers were not free to arrange the date. Wouldn't he have had to meet up with you at the dance?"

"That's true," she conceded thoughtfully. "We would have had to contrive a meeting at the same function, somehow ... and then hope for the best!" Instantly serious once more, she leaned forward. "Now you can begin to understand why the situation can be very trying for Julieta once she gets to Portugal. If she were pure Portuguese, endowed with only that nation's blood, the situation would have been vastly different—but, when all is said and done, there must also be much of her mother's, incorrigible, free spirit flowing though her veins!

"She may indeed have been raised strictly, but that side of her, the part that she inherited from her fun-loving mother, is already fighting to break free. One cannot expect otherwise. "And" (she wagged a slim forefinger for emphasis) "after having been reigned in for so long, she could become quite a handful!"

"Even in the office I have observed a subtle change in her, already. Her greatest ambition is, of course, to be exactly like the other girls."

"That's only natural" She shook her head emphatically. "One cannot too easily shake off one's background or upbringing, and who says that it is necessarily so desirable to be like the rest? Heaven alone knows, I am seriously concerned about today's youth. ... No, she will never be completely at home here, but we'll have to guard against such a radical change in her that she feels alien; uncomfortable when she's united with those of her own kin!"

I agreed wholeheartedly. Now I could well understand what Cameron Munroe was getting at when he had spoken so solemnly to me that day. When Angela Meiring asked me if I would be willing to use whatever influence I might have over Julieta to help her, I spontaneously promised to do everything in my power. Willy-nilly I was already allowing myself to be dragged deeper and deeper into this situation. If it ever became necessary to forbid the other girls on the staff to discuss their dates in her company, I was quite prepared to do so. I could not completely dampen their frivolous outlook on life, but if Julieta's happiness and her future within her father's family depended upon it, she would have to be disciplined very strictly.

When we left the table, we had coffee in the comparative cool of the Meirings' *stoep*[5], and as far as I was concerned, it was a really good visit. I sincerely liked this woman. She was friendly and almost childlike in her openness. Her ready use of my Christian name and the way in which she would carelessly mix her languages, created a delightfully informal atmosphere in a luxurious home which could so easily have been overwhelming.

We did not touch on the subject of Julieta again until it was almost time for me to leave. I could have lingered, because I was enjoying myself so much, but because I did not want to outstay my welcome on the occasion of my first visit,

---

5   Veranda

I rose just before 9:30, and, with a quick look at my wristwatch, rose and smoothed my skirt down over my hips.

"But, surely you don't want to go home yet!" she protested, to my gratification. "No. I shan't let you! Come, let's have another cup of coffee and then I'll go and pick you a bunch of sweet peas before you leave. I believe you have such a lovely flat, and you could surely use a few flowers, couldn't you?"

The end result was that I did not the leave there until after 10:30!

Explaining that the servants had long since gone to bed, she led me into the kitchen where she prepared the coffee herself. Among the gleaming white tiles and shiny pots and pans it was even less possible to be formal with one another.

I sighed. "What I would not do for a kitchen like this!"

"It is nice isn't it? Casper and I agree that, of all the rooms in this house, we like the kitchen best. When he originally began to talk about building a new house, I said, 'Cass, do whatever you want to do with the rest of the house, but you leave the kitchen to me! I want all the gadgets that money can buy!' ... I've not been the wife of a wealthy man all my life, Erin, and still have nightmares when I think of the primitive old kitchen we had on the farm; the dark brown paint on the walls, the miserably small windows and the gigantic coal stove on which I had to cook for the entire family on a suffocating, hot summer's day. Heavens no, never again!"

Before she went out into the garden to cut the flowers for me, she stopped suddenly, and exclaimed: "Hey, wait! Before I forget, there's something else I have to show you," and ran off to her bedroom to return a few minutes later with a letter which she handed to me to read.

"What do you think of this? It's from Ricardo, Julieta's cousin. The one in Portugal."

"The Marquis da Monsaraz?" I asked. "Cameron did tell me that he was the family's executor."

"He signs his correspondence simply as Ricardo da Monsaraz, but is known at home as 'the Marquis'. I doubt that that can be more than an honorary title now, and I also doubt that it is still hereditary, because since the revolution that custom has probably died out."

She turned on the *stoep* lights and took her flower basket with her, leaving me to read the letter alone in the kitchen so that I would have an opportunity to study the missive carefully.

He wrote in English; his handwriting and language equally faultless. I came to the conclusion that both the script and the wording were those of a proud, arrogant and unapproachable man. Then I remembered that when I had asked Cameron whether people like the marquis's grandmother still existed, he had promised to tell me about another such person. He had neglected to do so, but now it was not difficult for me to guess who that person could be. This Ricardo da Monsaraz was very clearly a faithful disciple of his grandmother; adhering to the same ideology.

He commenced the letter by thanking Mrs. Meiring for the kindness she had thus far shown Julieta, and then proceeded to assure her that it would not be necessary for her to keep the girl with her for very much longer. Her passport and other documents were now in order. Then two or three paragraphs followed, in which he very obviously searched for something more to say—references to unpleasant weather where he was, and so on—before I came to the part that Mrs. Meiring must have particularly intended for me to read.

"*It's completely unnecessary*," Ricardo da Monsaraz wrote, "*for this business to drag on for much longer.. Personally I shall be more than grateful to get it behind me as quickly as possible, and consequently I have applied in the correct circles for Julieta to be emancipated and declared an adult. According to data I received this morning from my lawyer, there seems to be hope that that will be arranged very shortly...!"*

"And what do you make of that?" my hostess asked when she came back. She wrapped the flowers carefully and set them down on the table beside me. "Is that kind of thing possible?"

"Oh yes! In many countries it certainly is. It's a complicated and involved business and I'm sure it would just confuse you if I went into details to explain it to you, using the legal terminology and so on, but briefly it just means that he is arranging to have our little friend 'emancipated' so that, in the eyes of the Portuguese court, she may soon be considered to be of age. Come...take an easy example. ... Imagine, or suppose I was only about 16 and were to be married outside of community property.—Automatically I would be considered 'of age'. I would now be completely responsible and, in addition, would be entitled to sign all manner of documents which I would not have been able to do before my marriage."

She still looked bewildered, so I explained further: "Property acquired by either spouse before their marriage is usually not considered marital property, so this would be done in order to protect Julieta's fortune in the event of her marriage. ... Emancipation means that she will be treated as an adult whatever the legal age is in Portugal. The term is used to describe the point in time when children no longer must answer to their parents, and parents are no longer responsible for their children. The children may be 'emancipated' by obtaining an 'emancipation decree' from the Juvenile Court in the county where they reside. It is a privilege, not a right, and is granted only to those minors who can demonstrate that they are prepared to live in the community like adults, but I am sure that the mighty marquis had no difficulty achieving that for our little friend; and of course, she was born in that country.—Property acquired by either spouse before their marriage is usually not considered marital property, which would protect Julieta's fortune in the event of her marriage. ... As I say, emancipation means that she will be treated as an adult whatever the legal age is in Portugal.—Does that make more sense?

"Well!" she smiled. "More or less. But it doesn't matter whether I understand or not.—The most important thing is that I now know that it is possible, because, from now onwards, until this has come through, I shall have to keep all the young blades, especially that the detestable Fernando, away from here!"

"Fernando?" I asked, surprised. "Fernando who? ... And what young blades?"

"Don't tell me she's never told you about Fernando Pereira? The pestilential, grasping, unscrupulous lout is there waiting for her almost every night when she gets home from work. He cares nothing for *her*, my dear. Without a doubt he has an ulterior motive."

At first I was surprised to hear that Julieta had any admirers of whom she had not told me, but, when I began to think about this, it became clear to me and I understood why she chose to remain silent about them. She was accustomed to being among people who were shocked when a young girl entered into a casual friendships with men. And, to make matters worse, when it came to Fernando, he had never even been formally introduced to her! Because her father had been killed while in the civil service, she received a small sum of money from the government every month, and Fernando was invariably the clerk who would pay this out to her. Furthermore, by this time, most of the officials in the local offices had become very well versed in all her personal affairs and present circumstances. It was quite possible, Angela explained to me as I inserted the key into the ignition of my car, that Fernando Pereira and the other clerks knew all too well about the fortune that awaited her if she measured up to Ricardo Monsaraz' ridiculous requirements.

"Perhaps he, Fernando, really likes her," I tried to console my new friend, and waved to her through the open window. "Thank you very much for a very pleasant evening and also for the lovely flowers."

"It was a pleasure," she called after me. "But don't forget ... over there you don't marry whom you choose, my dear. From what I've heard they choose a man for you, and if you don't like the gentleman, that's just too bad!"

Chapter Two

It was already the first Friday in February before I saw Angela Meiring again. She had actually come to see Cameron Monroe, but had then asked to be shown to my office as soon as her business with the lawyer was done. Julieta had already told me early that morning, when she had entered the building and had seen me at the elevator, that she had received another letter from her cousin, Ricardo, in which he informed her that his application had been granted and that he expected her to arrive in Portugal on the first possible vessel. Mrs. Meiring came to confirm the news for me.

"My dear Erin," she said with mock sympathy, "I'm afraid that you are about to lose your most valuable clerk. Before the end of this month you might well be saddled with a new understudy!"

"From the way you say that, Mr. Monroe has probably also told you about my particular mania!" I smiled and drew up a chair for her. "Sit down and chat for a moment. I'm dying of curiosity about this new development. Who thought this would happen so quickly!" As she removed her spotless white gloves and placed them carefully on top of the handbag on my desk, I added: "She is going home in two weeks' time. Did you know this?"

"Well, yes. I've just come back from the shipping agency. A cabin for two has been reserved for her on the *Santa Maria* which leaves on the 19th from Cape Town. Casper and I shall of course accompany her personally to Cape Town and see her safely on board...!"

"But why a *two-berth*?" I interrupted almost rudely. "Who's going with her?" For a wild moment I wondered if it was possible for a wedding still to take place within two weeks. It would have saved Da Monsaraz a great deal of trouble if he could have married her off a long time ago."

"I don't know as yet. That appears to be the only remaining fly in the ointment. Julieta has to have a chaperone. She can definitely not be permitted to travel alone. The august marquis would assuredly have a fit if she were to turn up on her own! ... I don't know about you, but I firmly believe in the value of a good first impression. I think that much depends upon that. If she has to go back there she might as well make a good start, don't you think?"

"I agree wholeheartedly, but where are you going to find a suitable companion so soon? What about checking with some of her parents' friends in LM? ... Perhaps one of them might be going, or know someone who is planning a trip to Portugal, and then she can meet up with that person.

"It would be very difficult to arrange at this stage, and one can't very well get on board a particular vessel just because friends of yours are among the passengers. What is more, it won't help to find someone who might immediately drop Julieta like a hot cake once she is safely in Portugal. The kid needs somebody who can be with her for a few months, stand sympathetically by her, and help her through what might turn out be a bewildering experience. A friend who will instill even minimal self-confidence in her, and, at the same time, tactfully discipline her. ... All expenses would of course be paid for the right person."

"Mmm, yes! I can see that now. In that case wouldn't it perhaps be better to advertise ..." I broke off sharply when I saw Julieta peeping in at the door. "Come in, my dear," I beckoned to her, and immediately turned my attention to Angela once more. "Some people would give their right hand for such an opportunity..." And perhaps it was because she saw that Mrs. Meiring was still with me, the child unceremoniously burst into my office, casting aside every vestige of self-discipline.

For some reason, throughout the course of our conversation I had been under the impression that there was something out of the ordinary in Angela Meiring's manner of speech, but had not succeeded very well in discerning what she had been hinting at; consequently I was totally unprepared when Julieta abruptly shot across the room and flung both her arms tightly around my neck,

"*You* must be the one who comes with me, my dearest... precious Erin!" she cried excitedly; and then added beseechingly. "*Please* come with me. I shan't ever be scared of Ricardo if you are there...!"

"**What**!" I almost yelled, struggling to break free of those eager young arms. "You don't know what you are talking about! Let go of me, you silly child, before you throttle me!"

But she was not prepared to give up so easily. Obediently, but not in the least penitent, she let go of me and went over to Angela. "What do you think, Auntie Angela?" she demanded of her. "Wouldn't that be wonderful? The ideal solution!"

"Actually it's not such a bad idea, now that I come to think of it, Erin," Angela replied thoughtfully—as if she really needed to give the matter serious consideration. I had to smile when I saw how hard she tried to pretend that the suggestion had only just occurred to her. "Man, upon further consideration I am inclined to regard this as an excellent idea. I'm sure that even Cameron would consider it time you had a really good holiday. Got away from the eternal office routine. I am certain that...!"

"You are both crazy!" I interrupted. "Quite mad!"

And that's precisely what Cameron said to me, shaking his head impatiently; hugely concerned about my new-found recklessness. "Nonsense! I have never known you to be like this!—So...so...*wild! What* has come over you lately?"

"But wasn't it you who personally recommended a visit to Portugal, not more than a week or two ago?" For the first time in all the years I had worked for him I was seated directly opposite him, in one of the chairs reserved for his clients. "I remind you of your exact words: 'If you want to see some wonderful old mansions and estates, encounter rare and noble courtesy and some of the most valuable antiques, family silver and priceless works of art, as well as examples of the most exquisite old lace in the world, you only have to journey through Portugal...' "

To my own astonishment I heard myself responding as though to a challenge. "I must escape before it is too late! The years are passing by too rapidly, and the bonds of habit are tightening more and more securely with every passing day.

"There are women on the staff who are older than I am and yet they almost make feel like their grandmother. Angela Meiring was right when she said it was high time I broke loose from office routine. I eat, sleep and drink court cases! ... I'm so busy helping to unravel other people's legal and matrimonial knots that I never have a chance to sort out my own problems. I live on the surface of reality. Like a parasite I feed off the affairs of others!"

Unconsciously my voice had been rising with every word I uttered until I suddenly realized that I was almost shouting at him. I was astounded at the bitterness in my words, and would probably have gone on ranting a good deal longer if the shocked expression on his face had not brought me to my senses.

"I am so sorry..." I began, cringing with embarrassment. "Please forgive me. I ... I ..." I was left gesturing wordlessly with my hands.

Because he looked so stunned, staring at me for so long after my outburst, I was convinced that I had well and truly overstepped the mark, but it then transpired that I had attributed the wrong explanation for the pain in his eyes. He moved quickly over to the door and closed it very deliberately. Then he came back slowly to stand so close to me that I had to look up in order to see his face.

This time it was my turn to be astonished. Because he had always been so tolerant, and so kind to me, I had long taken for granted his willingness to put up with my audacity and self-will. His patience had been nothing short of astounding. He had taken me out to dinner on several occasions after we had been obliged to work late in the office, and lately we had been to a few movies together, but I had never even begun to suspect...!

"You must have known, Erin," he protested when I told him this. "You must have guessed! Haven't you been able to wind me around your little finger right from the start?"

"But why have you never said anything before this? Why did you never tell me? It is unbelievable that any man could remain silent for so long about something like this! ... I mean... if you were so confident that I suspected, why did you never come out with it directly before today?"

"You gave me very little opportunity, my dear..."

That was perfectly true. I felt tears sting my eyes and impulsively I took his hand.

"I am overcome with more pride than I can ever express, Cam," I managed to murmur when I could trust my voice, "but I'm afraid I'm cut out to be an old maid." We smiled crookedly at one another and I tried to joke in order to dispel the awkwardness. "Perhaps after seeing all the 'lights and sights' of Europe, I'll be ready to subject my own determination to the stronger will of another!"

"On the other hand it might put you off matrimony forever to see how subservient the Monsaraz women are to their men folk" he responded, but a wry smile demonstrated that he was not serious. "Who knows, someday you may yet make an even better lawyer's wife than you ever were a secretary!"

This time I could answer his smile without any difficulty; grateful for the manner in which he had broken the tension. "Who knows?" I repeated, and then we began to discuss the particulars of my proposed voyage.—Yes, arrangements for my berth were already being made, as Mrs. Meiring had acquainted the marquis with my decision, and after some further discussion I made the suggestion that Suzanne Tredoux be trained to take my place.

"I'll have to give that some thought," he replied, screwing up his face so comically that I had to laugh. "Have you given any thought to what you might do with your flat[6]?"

This was a question I had dreaded because I knew what effect my response would have on him. When I told him that I intended selling everything in it, he could only blink his eyes in disbelief. He, of all people, knew too well what my home meant to me.

"What! Now I've heard everything! Have you taken leave of your senses, Erin? It almost sounds to me almost as though

---

6   Apartment

you do not plan to return—ever! Do you have your eye on a title, perhaps...or a *palacio* across the seas?"

"That'll be the day! Heaven preserve me!"

In truth it had cost me a few sleepless nights before coming to the agonizing decision to dispose of my precious furniture and my beloved little car, but, as I tried to explain to Cameron, I preferred to remain completely independent; regarding the actual voyage overseas, and all that might follow, as a holiday rather than a responsibility or an obligation.

Quite uncharacteristically I was determined not to concern myself too much about the future. After ten years of conscientious saving I'd accumulated quite a sizable sum of money in the bank, and I now thought it sensible to burn my bridges behind me.

"I'm most definitely determined to come back, Cam, but it would be impossible for me to relax for a moment if I were to be constantly concerned about what was happening to my stuff back home. The young people who are taking over my flat seem to be very nice, but nobody takes care of one's belongings the way you do, yourself. When they asked me if I would like to sell the furniture and everything else, as is, I was only too grateful."

Eventually he had to agree. "They're only *wêreldsgoed*—worldly possessions, as my dear mother used to say—and such things can sometimes become so important to one that they blind you to the other wonderful things that life holds."

Little did I know that I would some day regret the decision which would cut me off so completely from my old life!

It was a great relief to have the discussion with Cameron behind me, and when I left the office that afternoon, I began to be excited for the first time. Close to where I used to park my car every day, there was a music shop, and as I walked past it they just happened to be playing, inside, a melody that made my heart miss a beat, as it had done when I had first heard people like Louis Armstrong and Bing Crosby sing it some years before. I stood there completely transfixed, oblivious of the scores of people milling around me.

I was riveted to the spot as I tried to remember the title. ... The tune was so familiar that when, all at once, I again, heard a man's voice—Julio Eglesias, this time—singing the words, I could not help crying out exultantly: " *'Coimbra'*— *'April in Portugal*!'—This April I'll be there, myself!"

Chapter Three

I shall never forget my first journey along the *Tejo* to the harbor in Lisbon. The Tagus River—locally known as the *Rio Tejo*—forms part of the border between Portugal and Spain, and Lisbon is situated at the end of it on the north shore of the river.

My excitement which had already been kindled earlier, began to mount from the moment Estoril came into view. ... That beautiful place where the great casino is to be found, and where, as I'd heard from someone, the marquis had his villa. We sailed past a number of indescribably fine dwellings, and what struck me immediately was that there was not a single brick house to be seen among them, for all were stuccoed in bright colors. When we finally approached the *Belem* tower, a well-known landmark, I knew that the weeks of anticipation had come to an end.

We had arrived at our desired destination!

At the docks we were met by a tall, lean young man in an immaculate linen suit, whose manners were impeccable, and who introduced himself as Noël Estardos. He bowed low before us, almost low enough to dust the ground with his white Panama hat, declaring his regret for the fact that the

Marquis da Monsaraz had unexpectedly been called away that morning to the *palacio* in Sintra, where certain urgent matters awaited his attention. It was for this reason that he had sent him, Noël, his secretary, to be his unworthy replacement.

Addressing us in English—although Julieta spoke fluent Portuguese and I had already begun to understand a few words—he welcomed us in the most effusive terms. Thereafter he grabbed a suitcase in each hand and walked ahead to the magnificent limousine awaiting us outside, graciously invited us to get into it and then undertook to see to our luggage; at which stage I was only too pleased to hand over our tickets, and gratefully sank back into luxurious depths of the seats.

The 'unworthy replacement' did not take leave of us before once again unnecessarily begging our pardon—this time for the vehicle...'this soapbox'...the 'horse-cart' in which he was obliged to transport us to our hotel! The worthy marquis, he explained, had himself driven his private car to Sintra.

Behind the pristine white back, Julieta and I smiled delightedly at one another, watching him until he disappeared into the depths of the customs building to take over all responsibility for our well-being. Somehow we could not refrain from giggling, and I thought of Angela Meiring. How she would have enjoyed all this. I, myself, felt ten years younger than when I had hung over the ship's railing to bid farewell to Table Bay not too long before.

How can I ever do justice to a description of my first journey through the streets of Lisbon with its tree-ringed public squares? The lush green of the foliage and the riotous profusion of flowers on the shrubs that grew everywhere. ... The sunlight and shadows under the trees on the sidewalks...!

Here, as along the banks of the Tagus, the houses were painted in vivid colors; in shades of red, yellow or blue, and that, in addition to the bright colors worn by the people, could very well cause a visitor to wonder if the dawn of every new day did not herald another festivity of some sort.

Julieta, who had been unusually quiet while her dark eyes were solemnly taking in the highlights of the city, confessed to me in a small voice, just before we drew up in front of our hotel, that it scared her to realize how little she remembered of the place. I could only squeeze her hand sympathetically for a moment, and then Noël was opening the car door for us.

Her mercurial nature rendered it impossible for her to remain downhearted for very long, however, and that it was never difficult for her regain her customary self-confidence, was especially noticeable in the company of the opposite sex. Before we had been at the hotel for more than a quarter-hour both she and I could detect a decided flicker of interest in Noël's black eyes, and, thus encouraged, Julieta began to sparkle.

At that moment I longed for nothing more than a nice, tepid bath and clean clothes, because although it was still early April, and only the beginning of Spring, the humidity made it suffocatingly warm; but with all that Angela Meiring and Cameron Monroe had instilled in me concerning Portuguese propriety and social conduct, still fresh in my memory, I did not consider it advisable to leave Julieta alone in the company of a young man. Consequently I could only sit there resignedly sipping the syrupy-sweet black coffee which the waiter had brought us, and disinterestedly listen, with one ear, to the voices of the other two. It was difficult to make out everything that they were saying; and when the humidity eventually made that task too exhausting, I stared through the window and gave my thoughts free reign.

I could hardly believe that I was really there, that it was April, and that the city that stretched out before my dreamy gaze was indeed Lisbon. It was almost unbelievable, and it would take me a long time before I would become used to the knowledge that someone else was now sitting at *my* desk, in *my* office, that there were strangers in *my* flat, and that others were now able to wander around, watching—through *my* windows—the lights of Johannesburg begin to blink like so many bright, friendly eyes, each evening after sundown!

So far everything had proceeded without a hitch and, except for the incident with Fernando Pereira, there was nothing I had cause to regret. With a part of my attention still fixed on Julieta and Noël, I thought again of Pereira, and wondered if he would ever find out how neatly we had outwitted him. (He was the dubious character whom Angela had described as that 'grasping, unscrupulous lout'—the clerk who would pay out to Julieta the pension due to her after her father's death, and who had consequently managed to become so well versed in all her personal affairs and present circumstances.)

A wise woman, Angela Meiring, I decided. Little escaped her notice, and she definitely had the gift of being able to size up people the moment she met them. Just as she had feared, the scoundrel had gradually become more and more persistent. When he discovered that Julieta was at long last going back to Portugal, he had clearly put two and two together, and suddenly become ever so attached to her! In fact he had gone as far as to inform Angela that he wanted to marry the child, and had asked her to obtain the necessary permission from Ricardo da Monsaraz.

I naturally wondered how much Julieta knew about any of this. Could Fernando possibly still be orthodox enough to have waited for the desired permission before declaring his feelings to the girl? Sitting there in a Lisbon hotel I decided that it no longer made much difference. We had set a trap for him and he had neatly walked into it. By his own conduct he had proved that even our worst suspicions had not been unfounded...

When the staff had decided that, before Julieta and I left the office for the last time, they should arrange a small farewell party for us in my flat, if I would permit it, they must have known that obtaining the required permission was a foregone conclusion, and it was when Cameron Monroe made the suggestion that Fernando Perez should also be invited, that the four of us, (for Angela's husband, Casper Meiring, was now included) hatched a conspiracy.—We planned to get Perez out onto my balcony on some pretext or another and then casually drop the information that Julieta was no longer going to inherit any part of her grandmother's estate. We optimistically reckoned that, seeing me alone on the balcony at some stage during the evening, Fernando would see fit to join me. When that did indeed happen, I was able to tell myself, with great satisfaction, that everything was already going off better than we had anticipated, but a surprise awaited me. It would soon appear what we had so far taken as a joke, was a hundred times more serious than we could have dreamed!

For a few moments Fernando and I remained silent, looking out over the Golden city; then he cleared his throat nervously. "You have a very beautiful flat, Miss March," he remarked. "I understand from Julieta that you had an exceptionally good position with Mr. Monroe?"

I wondered where this was leading. It was so clearly more a rhetorical question than a declaration, but what kind of response was he hoping for? The man just generally rubbed me up the wrong way. I did not like him one bit; thus, when I met his expectant gaze, I had an inner desire to ask him what on earth that had to do with him. Instead, I smiled sweetly.

"Yes I think it was a very good position ... or rather, it was a very pleasant job."

"Now you're trying to avoid my question, dear lady!"

So far the conversation was not proceeding along our pre-determined lines. I was decidedly not *his* dear lady. "I'm extremely sorry, Mr. Pereira," I responded stiffly, "but I really don't know what you mean."

The next moment he had me shaking with rage. "Oh yes you do!" he protested emphatically. "You know well enough. To give up as much as you have, you must be very firmly convinced that all this is going to be well worth your while!"

"*How dare you!*" I could hardly rely on my voice, and it was only with the greatest difficulty that I conquered the shaking of my hands. Never before had I had such a fervent desire to slap someone.

"Oh come now!" Remaining completely cool, and not put off in any way, he regarded me amusedly. "Let us understand one another. How strong is your influence over Julieta? If you and I can come to a satisfactory arrangement and work this out well enough, we can both make a packet out of it!"

As I had no intention of listening to another word, I swung around angrily and was just about to go back inside when, to my great relief, I saw Cameron in the doorway, with a glass in his hand.

"I have come to look for you in order to bring you a drink, Erin. ... "But why do you look so upset?" Smiling questioningly he glanced from me to Fernando.

Breathless, but now completely calm, I took the glass from him and turned to look triumphantly at Perez.

"I was just about to tell Fernando the bad news about Julieta. I think it is absolutely scandalous!"

"What news about Julieta?" the scoundrel demanded promptly, just as I knew he would.

"So Miss March has not yet told you?" Cameron asked— exactly as I had hoped he would do. "The poor child no longer has a hope in Hades of getting a cent out of her grandmother's estate. The cousin—that cad, the marquis—is about to cheat her out of everything, and there is absolutely nothing she can do about it!"

"But ... but surely she is not going to sit back with folded hands and allow this!" Fernando stammered.. *"This ... this... this is decidedly criminal!* She must do something!"

"As you are well aware, Mr. Munroe is a himself lawyer," I put in, "and he has already ascertained that Julieta is in no position to provide a single, well-grounded argument," I lied unashamedly. "According to the will, all decisions rest entirely with Ricardo da Monsaraz. ... He can do just as he pleases!" (At least this much was true!)

"Yes," Cameron added, with ill-disguised glee. "She's off to Portugal, possibly to become nothing more than a servant in her cousin's ménage. The man says that she will be treated like a daughter in his house, but ..." he shrugged his shoulders.

"That's why I'm selling everything!" I explained—now on a 'roll' and laughing inwardly. "I need to have the money to cover my expenses because I really cannot just 'sit back,' as you put it, and see that innocent child go there all alone with no one to see to it that she is treated fairly. Ask Mr. and Mrs. Meiring ... they're just as concerned!"

It was a shameless skunk, absolutely crushed, that I left behind on the balcony with Cameron.

When I re-entered the living room, I winked conspiratorially at the Meirings. Julieta, who had seen me return, immediately came over and drew her arm through mine to lead me towards the buffet.

"Where have you been hiding all this time" she asked reproachfully. "I was afraid that you were not enjoying our party."

"Oh, just having a last look at Johannesburg," was my airy explanation.

Just then my musings were interrupted as I was drawn back to the present by the sound of Julieta's voice. "*Señorita* Erin, *Señhor* Estardos is about to depart. Did you not hear him bid you *adeus*?"

Feeling somewhat sheepish I extended my hand to him. "Please forgive me, *Señhor!* We were up very early this morning and the climate is making me a little drowsy. I was daydreaming..."

Exhibiting characteristic courtesy he bowed over my moist hand.

"*Adeus, minha Señorita* March. Before I depart, please permit me to convey the marquis's good wishes, once more, as well as the message that he will visit you as soon as he returns!"

The moment he disappeared down the stairs, I ran to my room and grabbed hold of the suitcase I had brought with me from the car.

"Now I intend to find some clean clothes, my little friend," I said to Julieta, "and then I am going to have a bath. Please ring that bell for the chambermaid and ask her where the nearest bathroom is to be found."

Thus far I have neglected to explain that, with a eye to our individual futures, I had deemed it unwise to book into an hotel that was too expensive. As it later turned out, the one of our choice was far from luxurious and, for that reason, largely favored by students who demanded nothing more than a place to sleep, and three heaped plates of food every day. There was only one bathroom on every floor. In ours there was a tap that invariably screeched, groaned and spluttered, rattling the pipes before it would reluctantly spit out a few drops of tepid water.

As I was leaving our bedroom with my clothes and a fresh towel draped over my arm, Julieta observed thoughtfully: "You know, *Señorita* Erin, I cannot refrain from wondering why Fernando did not come to take leave of me in Johannesburg as he promised. It is fortunate that he has my address here, and also that of Ricardo's villa in Estoril. He will probably write soon to enlighten me...!"

Aboard the *Santa Maria* I had become quite accustomed to oil in my food. I had even decided that the addition of a little olive oil actually improved a salad. Cabbage undoubtedly seemed to remain crisp for a longer period. But, after an enormous plate of thick cabbage soup on such a stifling day, sardines in oil were a bit much for me.

We ate in silence, acutely aware of the many eyes focused upon us. Because there were so many young men in the dining room—most likely students—I kept a strict eye on Julieta.

"It is at you that they are staring," she giggled when she suddenly saw through my stern, watchful attitude. "They have probably never seen a genuine blonde before! Come on, *Señorita*. Smile back!"

Not flattered in the least, because I knew only too well what effect that dark, glossy hair and those mischievous eyes could have on eager young men, I pursed my lips and tried to look as much like a formidable chaperone as I possibly could.

After the meal, drowsiness descended like a heavy blanket upon the hotel, and, as we climbed the stairs again, I said to Julieta, "It may well be my duty to see to it that you lie down and rest for a while, but I, personally, shall not be taking a siesta until I have bought myself a bottle of Lavender water." My hair clung to my forehead in damp curls, and I longed for the cool refreshment of my favorite kind.

After managing to locate a pharmacy it transpired that the word 'perfume' was well understood by the assistant but 'Lavender' was beyond him. He brought to light a variety of exquisite bottles containing overwhelming, exotic perfumes, but I could not be tempted even to smell any one of them. Who could do so after those sardines and in such heat, without feeling nauseous?

"Yardley's," I attempted at last, to the great amusement of the other people in the store, and peered through the gloom in a attempt to ascertain whether what I sought might not perhaps be hiding somewhere in one of the glass-fronted showcases.

"*Yardley's?* " I tried again, hopefully. In vain!

The sallow young clerk and I were equally startled when a man who had probably been waiting his turn for quite a few minutes, suddenly stepped forward and amusedly said: "Lavender! ... *Alfazema*!"

While somewhat surprised that a Portuguese gentleman would know that, I was, of course, highly delighted when I finally obtained what I wanted. I smiled gratefully at the stranger. *"Obrigado!* Thank you very much, *Señhor!"*

When the shop assistant named the price I was none the wiser, and I must uncertainly have glanced at the helpful stranger as I opened my purse, produced a handful of change and then extended my hand, because, without a word, he quite casually selected the necessary coinage from my open palm. Everyone who had followed the proceedings with interest, so far, bowed in unison, and came closer in case he was about to do me another favor.

"There now, *Señorita*," he said, with a particularly attractive grin, "you see, that it is very simple if one is not too proud to ask!"

I thanked him again and walked out with the smile still on my face ... I could not wait to relate the occurrence to Julieta, but when I realized that the man from the shop was following me, my excitement evaporated; and when he suddenly called out to me, my shoulders stiffened with fear.

"*Señorita!* ... Please. ... Wait!"

This request made me walk even more quickly. Then he shouted: "Please wait, *Señorita!* ... Miss March!"

To say that I nearly fainted is no exaggeration. The sheer astonishment on my face when I swung round must have appeared very comical to him, for he suddenly stopped dead in his tracks on the sidewalk, and laughed so uproariously that passersby also stopped to look at us.

"Don't ... know when ... I last had such fun! Are you wondering whether I might perhaps be clairvoyant or something?"

"Oh," I gasped with relief, and although his use of a word like 'fun' seemed out of character, I managed to respond with: "Then you must be...?"

"No!" And he favored me with that disarming smile once more. "I am not! The formidable Ricardo is my cousin, too. I am Carlos ... merely another of the poor relatives." He smiled wryly. "Like the fair Julieta I am also waiting impatiently for a few escudos to come my way!"

There was something so likeable in the man's face; in the blue eyes that met mine so trustingly under black brows—and so unexpected in that pleasant swarthy face —that it was as though we had known one another for years!

After we had remained chatting on the sidewalk for a while he took me by the arm and led me out into the street. "We can't possibly stand here and bake in the sun for much longer. Let's go and find a café and see if, in this impossible place, they serve things like cold drinks!"

This of course reminded me of the fact that he did not usually reside in Portugal. I recalled what Cameron had told me about Carlos; particularly that his father had married a Scottish girl.

"But what about Julieta?" I protested, and consulted my wristwatch.

"Forget her!" He laconically brushed aside my concern. "She knows that I've come to look for you and will bring you back safely.—And you don't have to be concerned about her going out alone or doing anything silly while she's alone. ... She's not a baby, and when I left her, she was very busy unpacking her suitcases." Undeterred, he walked on purposefully; his arm persuasively hooked through mine.

"Come on. ... We have to celebrate your arrival in Lisbon. Just sorry that I'm unable to place a posh automobile like cousin Ricardo's at your disposal. Sadly, any woman who is willing to put up with my company, will also have to be prepared to footslog.

"My autocratic and straight-laced cousin simply cannot condone my way of life. If he could see us now, he would probably pass out from sheer shock!"

I really felt like saying. "To heck with Ricardo!" or something equally rude, but fortunately restrained myself. Instead I sat listening intently to all that Carlos had to tell about himself.

It surprised me to learn that he was still a student, or at least that he was engaged in advanced study. He had apparently attained several degrees, among them one in architecture, and was now busy working towards a doctorate. "That money from grandmother Monsaraz will certainly come in very handy," he added matter-of-factly.

"That I can well believe." Inwardly it made my blood boil just think of Ricardo Monsaraz. Who was he to monitor the lives of others and to control their futures? The more I heard about the man, the less I liked him. I saw him in my imagination as proud, narrow-minded, perpetually scowling, not very pleasant to look at and completely devoid of any sense of humor. It was easy to picture him as a sort of cruel 'circus ringmaster', who could pull strings whenever he wanted Julieta and Carlos to dance for his amusement! My indignation mounted when Carlos described all he had given up when he was obliged to cancel his entry to the Scottish university in order to come to Portugal.

"I was fortunate enough to find an opportunity to lecture at a college in Coimbra, because, having a fixed salary makes things a lot more comfortable for me during my stay here! But Erin, I'm like a fish out of water here! Just like Julieta, having lived here for a only a short period in the past, I'm already homesick. I long for the heather where I grew up. I'm like a fish out of water in this place and there is nobody who cares about whether I live or die!"

"Poor Carlos!" My sympathy was sincere. "Julieta has a lot to be grateful for. Her case is completely different. In Lourenco Marques she was raised very much like any young girl here. It is only since the death of her parents that she has been allowed such freedom, and now she can sometimes be very rebellious. If she feels like it, and if the marquis approaches her in the wrong way, she's quite capable of telling him to go to pot!"

Carlos threw his head back and laughed heartily. "Would she really? Then she's a girl after my own heart. We evidently have a lot in common." He cocked his head to one side for a moment, as if he should reconsider what he had just said, and then, with a broad grin, he added: "No. There is one *big* difference between us. I would think twice before I would say that to him!"

Sitting under a striped umbrella, amid shady trees in that outdoor café, we came to know one another quite well and, in due course, Carlos asked me how it happened that Julieta and I had become friends. "To me," he said, "you appear to be the furthest from a stern chaperone that I've ever come across," he remarked amusedly. "But I must say, it's wonderful to find, in this place, this relic of the Middle Ages, a girl with whom I can at least be myself. We have hardly known one another for half an hour and here I am already calling you by your first name!"

I also had to admit that it was a surprise to me after what I had expected, but secretly I found it rather nice to be referred to as a 'girl,' and I assured him that I was prepared to mind my p's and q's for Julieta's sake. I told him the whole story, starting with the first time I saw Julieta. Of the rascal, Fernando, I made no mention at all.

"In my opinion it is very decent of you to come just because of compassion for somebody else," he then said, to my great embarrassment—and my explanation that I had also longed to see foreign places didn't seem to make very much difference. He simply added: "I wish I had somebody like you to take care of me and see to it that I am not shortchanged. My part of the situation has thus far not run smoothly, that I can assure you."

Upon again consulting my watch, I jumped up in some consternation and, grabbing my purse I had to say, "Please excuse me, Carlos. Thank you for everything, but I really must go now. Can it be three-thirty already? I can't believe that time has gone by so quickly!"

"I shall regard that as a compliment, *Señorita* March," he responded, favoring me with an obsequious, exaggerated bow.

As we walked back to the hotel as quickly as possible, I was thankful that Carlos had been sent to look for me. Without him I would never again have found the place. All the streets looked exactly the same to me, and it was thus with a certain degree of surprise that I suddenly found myself back at the Hotel Estrêla once more.

Parked beside the curb at the entrance was a cream-colored *La Gonda*[7] with red leather upholstery and an impressive coat of arms beside the handles of the two front doors.

"Oh!" commented Carlos, somewhat taken aback. 'It appears that my illustrious cousin, the marquis, has returned in our absence."

---

7   **Lagonda:** a luxury four-door saloon built by Aston Martin between 1976 and 1989. A total of 645 were produced at an average selling price of £150,000. The name was derived from the Lagonda marque that Aston Martin had purchased in 1947.

Chapter Four

I could find no acceptable reason for feeling like a naughty schoolgirl, or a little girl caught with her fingers in the cookie jar. It was after all Julieta, not I, who was being put to the test! As long as I kept her in check I would be performing my duties. Nevertheless, as I opened the door of the small sitting room on our floor, I realized that my curiosity was mingled with a considerable degree of nervousness, and I steeled myself; determined that the marquis would not be permitted to intimidate me. I smiled encouragingly at Carlos and entered the room with my head held high.

Julieta relieved the tension by coming to meet me, and grabbing me by my arm.

"Oh Erin, I'm so pleased that Carlos found you! Allow me to introduce my cousin, the Marquis Ricardo da Monsaraz. ... Ricardo, my dear friend, *Señorita* Erin March."

Before the marquis bent over my hand, as I was by now able to anticipate that he would, I was aware only of a well-built man with broad shoulders; far more handsome than any man had a right to be, and with a magnificent head of almost blue-black hair. Once we were all seated, I did, however, have an opportunity to study him more closely, and I came to the conclusion that, as far as his appearance was concerned, he was, in most other ways, precisely as I had pictured him. ... A dark, proud face, sculptured features, a broad forehead and a mouth and chin that could have been cast in steel. Decidedly not the countenance of a person who would condone (or readily forgive) weakness in another; unyielding in his almost fanatical expectation that others should respect and adhere to his principles.

I had a further opportunity to study Ricardo da Monsaraz while his attention was fixed on the other two. Carlos, talking far too much, related how he had found me and persuaded me to have a cold drink with him, omitting any amusing details and carefully providing only such as were essential.

Elegantly clad in an impeccable, light grey tailored suit, a white shirt and a conservative maroon tie, there was nothing foppish or 'dandified' as one might have expected from one such as he. He, Da Monsaraz, listened attentively, if thoughtfully, while in no way relaxing that arrogance. That impassive face in which every feature could have been carved out of granite—(I soon ran out of applicable similes!) was as unlovable as I had expected—but I could not in all honesty permit myself to deny that it was, at the same time, the face of a man who would, at all costs, see justice done.

That made me feel a good deal better. Rather such a man to have to deal with than a despot who would allow his personal feelings about another to influence his own.

So deeply lost in thought was I that it was with a start that I realized that he was addressing me. His dark eyes narrowed, he was looking intently at me.

"I must apologize for the thoughtlessness of my cousin, *Señorita*," he said with cool, impersonal courtesy. "I can only offer his lack of familiarity with the standards of his family as an excuse for his reckless conduct. ... It is unthinkable for a man to have taken a respectable young lady to such a public place, alone!"

"But Ricardo..." Carlos began, his face as red as a beetroot.

"That is enough!" Da Monsaraz responded emphatically, with a gesture to indicate that the subject was closed. "Let us hear no more about this. I fear that we shall bore the ladies!" He turned benevolently to Julieta. "It grieves me, my dear young cousin, that you and your charming friend (favoring me fleetingly with a cool smile) should find yourselves in such an uncongenial place as this. I am astonished to have come upon you unpacking your own valises. ... Surely there must be a servant who can perform such duties for you, or is your chambermaid unwilling do to that?"

"I am quite used to doing things like that for myself, Ricardo," Julieta protested, smiling; but for me what had already transpired was beyond endurance. How dared he belittle Carlos in this way? The man's conceit was just too much!

To my surprise I heard myself say: "Pardon me, *Dom* Ricardo, but it is no more than fair that I should explain that I accompanied Carlos of my own free will!"—The familiarity with which I referred to Carlos must have shocked him, but with practiced self-control he did not move a muscle.—"I am well aware of the customs of your people, and, in particular, with the standards of your family, as you expressed not long ago, and I respect them, but as I am not a Portuguese lady they consequently have little bearing upon my personal conduct. ... On the other hand I shall be very careful to see to it that Julieta conducts herself with decorum and propriety, and, when she is with me, my conduct will be exemplary, but I cannot permit my own movements to be restricted. By gratefully accepting a friendly invitation such as that extended by Carlos, on such a stifling day, I did nothing that would be frowned upon were I at home, and Carlos knew that!"

If I intended this outburst to put him in his place and shake him from his almost imperturbable calm, I certainly did not succeed. As I stammered on and on incoherently, breathless—and saying far more than I intended—I only began to feel more and more like a clumsy schoolgirl. I could have cried from sheer exasperation when his expression remained completely unruffled.

"That may be so, and I find your explanation interesting," he responded impassively, sounding bored more than anything else, "and I do not doubt that you were speaking the truth, but I cannot regard Carlos' conduct with anything but disgust. Now, if you will excuse me, I must take my departure as I am expecting guests for dinner. I have already arranged with Julieta that my chauffeur will be here early tomorrow morning to fetch you, as both you—and she—will be my guests in Estoril. I shall also send another vehicle to take your heavy luggage, such as trunks, to my permanent residence. *Adeus Señoritas!* ... Come, Carlos, I shall drop you off at the railway station!"

As furious as I was, I would have been lacking in courtesy if I permitted the two men to leave without seeing them off. Julieta and I went on ahead, and when we all reached the foyer of the hotel our group caused quite a sensation. The manner in which people waiting there made way for us would have been amusing, if I had not been too angry to enjoy the situation. Clearly the family crest on Ricardo da Monsaraz' car was more impressive than I had thought.

As Carlos greeted me I noticed that the attractive smile had given way to one of wry embarrassment, and as I was immediately able to interpret the barely visible shrug of his shoulders, sympathy for him overcame me to the extent that I took leave of the marquis I could hardly manage more than a stiff: "Good afternoon, *Señhor* Da Monsaraz!"

"Well, what did you think of our stunning Ricardo?" Julieta demanded, the moment we were back in our room. "Isn't he just too adorable?" In her customary, excitable manner she talked ceaselessly, making it difficult to believe that she actually drew breath. "I think he's the handsomest man I've ever seen in my life!

"Of course he is completely beyond my reach.—In any case he's a bit on the old side for me, don't you think? .... Carlos is more my match. ... Isn't Ricardo absolutely too wonderful for words? The whole time he was here I felt as if I was taking part in a movie. ... I wonder..."

"I think he is just about the most detestable man it has ever been my misfortune to meet!" I finally managed to interrupt her. "He makes me sick!"

"I expected you to say that," she commented dryly, to my astonishment. "You just can't bear it that any man should get the better of you, Erin, *querida!* After all, I saw how you wiped the floor with Cameron Monroe," she continued, exhibiting insight never revealed before. "It's going to be very entertaining to see how you and Ricardo are going to get on.—Steel versus marble, and the one as inflexible as the other!"

"Julieta, you dear, silly little fool," I laughed, in a good mood once more. "You may appear to be an inexperienced 'babe-in-arms' but, heaven knows, to me you are a revelation!"

Recalling that Carlos had told me that, in Portugal, the closest equivalent of the South African four o'clock 'teatime' would be at about 5:30, as had been the custom aboard the *Santa Maria*, and I told her that. Usually coffee or wine were also served, and visitors would then be treated to an overwhelming variety of cookies, cakes and tarts. I doubted that that would be the case in the hotel.

"You'll just have to stick it out," I told her callously, teasing her but then relenting. "I think I'd be able to find the place where I was with Carlos this afternoon, without too much difficulty. They have the most excellent lime cordial there, or perhaps we could even get tea."

"Oh, let's go, Erin!" she pleaded enthusiastically. "I haven't even been out of the hotel since we arrived and I so badly want to see what the shops are like!"

Ten minutes later the two of us were walking about like any other regular tourists, viewing the buildings and streets in the area with great interest.

"We're here!" observed Julieta in wonderment. "We're here, *really* here, Erin! We're going to have a wonderful holiday, you and I. Please be nice to Ricardo because he can take us about in that marvelous *La Gonda* of his."

"I shall try," I promised with a smile, "but I still maintain that he is the last person on earth whom I would describe as ... what did you call him again? Oh yes... 'adorable!' "

Her youthful enthusiasm and zest for living were so infectious that it wasn't difficult to get into the same, carefree holiday spirit. I could afford to be indulgent towards this young girl. ... Wasn't it through her that I had been rescued from the old groove of habit and soul-destroying routine? ... Consequently I made up my mind to be as pleasant as possible towards the annoying Ricardo, for her sake. Suddenly I sincerely hoped that my behavior that afternoon would not be to her detriment..

"But he *was* a bit unfair to Carlos, don't you think, Julieta?" I asked her thoughtfully after we had found the café we sought. "Ricardo, I mean. He didn't even give him a chance to say whether he wanted to go or stay. When the high and mighty marquis announced that he would take him to the station in his car, he had no option but to leave."

"Yes, that's true," she conceded pensively. "I really like Carlos. He makes me laugh. ... Wasn't it kind of him to come and welcome us?"

"It was, indeed. You two are in the same boat and he probably wanted to show you that you can depend on him if you find too many obstacles in the way. I wonder how he knew where to find us."

"Apparently Aunt Luisa had told him that we were expected," she explained, "and as soon as he arrived in Lisbon, he phoned Noël Estardos and asked him at which hotel we would be staying. Ricardo probably won't be too pleased with his secretary when he learns *that!*" She giggled mischievously. "By the way, Carlos tells me that my dear aunt has her eye on Ricardo.—Isabella, her eldest daughter is now a widow and decidedly back in the marriage Market!"

Chapter Five

For many years—ever since I had read in a Johannesburg newspaper about the wedding of one of Portugal's princesses that had taken place there—I had longed to visit Estoril. For some reason, perhaps because I had long associated it with that article, the very name of the place inevitably triggered in my imagination an impression of enchantment and romance; of golden sunshine and wealth. It was there that members of the nobility and other famous personages from all corners of the earth, would gather to spend a holiday. It was quite possible that, if we went to the casino, we would see one or more of Hollywood's idols in the flesh, and consequently, despite my aversion to the pompous marquis, I looked forward to my stay at his villa.

As has already been said, our luggage had been brought from the docks on the previous afternoon, before the arrival of Carlos and the marquis, and after I had unpacked the most necessary of my belongings, I chose one of my favorite dresses and carefully ironed it. According to my friends, the brilliant blue of the gorgeous material made my skin glow, my eyes seem darker, and lent more color to my face—altogether a most desirable effect, if I could rely on their opinion! What I did know for sure, however, was that the fullness of the skirt unfailingly made me feel ready even for a garden party, and consequently happy and self-confident.

I dressed very carefully. With an eye to the possibility of a promenade along the beachfront, and, in case the heat might be nigh unbearable at midday, I chose to wear a white hat with a wide brim, and my best white shoes to complete the outfit. White gloves were tucked into my purse in the event that the marquis could possibly take us to some formal place, where he might consider them essential.

When I looked through a window in our bedroom, coincidentally just as a familiar, cream-colored car drew up in front of the hotel entrance downstairs, I began to look forward to the day with happy anticipation and great excitement. I felt as young and carefree as Julieta, who looked charming in a frock of white *broderie anglaise* which she wore with red shoes and a broad red sash.

The fact that the marquis did not come personally but, as he had promised, had sent his chauffeur to fetch us, was not in any way, a disappointment. As a matter of fact we were delighted. There can certainly be few other experiences as exciting as climbing into a limousine as imposing as that of Ricardo da Monsaraz, and have a liveried chauffeur stand at attention while holding the door open for you. As the car glided forward like a gracious swan the hotel porter saluted us, and Julieta and I laughed to see all the curious faces looking down at us out of the hotel windows!

Any fear I had harbored concerning my behavior on the previous evening proved to have been unnecessary. It did not appear to have had an adverse effect on Da Monsaraz' attitude towards his young cousin. From the outset it was clear that he was wholly taken with her. He enjoyed teasing her good naturedly, and smiled with gentle amusement at her precocious observations.

It was strange but, somehow, now that I was to be his guest, I, too, was treated with all the considerable courtesy that was habitually extended to his visitors. His attitude towards Julieta was more that of an indulgent father or proud uncle. Have I not already said that, in the early days of our relationship, Julieta had reminded me of a cute, playful kitten? Well, that is probably how the marquis saw her.

Cameron Munroe had told me a great deal about Portuguese courtesy. The change in Ricardo da Monsaraz was, however, almost beyond belief! In his own home he was charm and kindness personified. I had not been in his company for more than five minutes before I came to the conclusion that one needed to see him in the rôle of host to get to know him. It was hard to believe that this friendly, hospitable person, was the same man who had, on the previous afternoon, seemed almost to be my enemy. Furthermore, whoever was motivated to describe that magnificent residence with its broad marble steps and tiled patios as a 'villa' must, without a doubt, have been a master in the art of understatement. My first thought, for obvious reasons was: "If this is his villa, I can't wait to see the *palacio!*"

Even before the car came to a stop, *Dom* Ricardo appeared on the steps. In his yachting blazer and wearing a white open-necked shirt he seemed a lot younger than at our previous meeting. Once more I could hardly believe my eyes when he went over to Julieta, who was the first to get out of the car, and kissed her lightly on her cheek. It's wonderful how clothes can influence one's behavior, was my rather cynical observation, and anyone who wishes to disagree needs only to bear in mind how difficult it is to feel dignified in a bathing suit!

I was also welcomed very warmly. He solicitously wanted to know if he hadn't sent the car, too early for us, if we had found the short journey enjoyable, and if I wasn't perhaps homesick already.

"We shall have to see to it that you feel quite at home and happy here, *Señorita*," he said with charming courtesy and, walking ahead, chatted nonstop in order to make us feel at home.

It was almost impossible to take it all in at once. The general impression was one of cool spaciousness. Grace, comfort, and superb taste were cleverly combined so that the place was beautifully furnished, without any pretentiousness which would decidedly have spoiled the holiday atmosphere of Estoril. Effective use of light, and enormous windows, lent the impression that the ocean could be right there in the house. It was almost as though one were outside on the beach, with the foam in one's face, and yet could, at the same time, sit comfortably and relax in the shade. The marquis seemed pleased when I admired the exquisite small tiles with which the walls as well as the floor of a glass-roofed atrium—complete with lily pond—had been laid out.

"We call them *azulejos*," he explained. "One day when you and Julieta come to Sintra I must arrange for you to visit the small factory I have there, and see how they are made."

"That I would like very much," I replied with unfeigned eagerness.

"I have requested José to prepare a table out of doors so that we can enjoy our refreshments on the North side of the house," he informed us after we had spent a few minutes leaning over the pond to watch the fish, and then he led us through a wide glass door. "Unfortunately there is no view of the sea from here, but I always find it the coolest place at this time of the year."

It was indeed a delightful spot, with a wealth of brightly-hued and scented shrubs, among them Oleander and Jasmine, and where we sat in the shade of a gigantic tree the air was heavy with the perfume of Frangipani, Camphor, Patchouli, and others which I was unable to identify until the marquis listed them for me. The dreamlike unreality of the situation became even more unreal for me when our host remarked, with the first smile I had yet seen on that normally impassive face: "Julieta has told me how you have complained about all the coffee you have had to imbibe since leaving South Africa, *Señorita* March. I have thus seen to it that a pot of tea be prepared especially for you."

I am completely unable to describe the sparkling 'whiteness' which briefly lit up the somber face, in any other way than 'overwhelming!' Then, having been rendered speechless for a moment, I found myself compelled to respond, and I somehow heard myself saying: "The entire trip from Lisbon has now become worthwhile *Señor Marquis*," speaking as if there had never been a 'yesterday afternoon!'

Shortly before lunch another vehicle arrived at the villa, and then, for the first time in more than fifteen years Julieta became acquainted once more with her aunt—*Tia Luisa* as they called her—and her cousin, the young Countess Isabella da Silva. Mario, another cousin and the driver of the car, she did not know at all.

It was an elegant, if hardly jolly group among whom we sat down to lunch ... and what a meal that was! A luncheon that Julieta described as "Out of this world!" Later, during my stay in the *palacio*, I would have to battle with a banquet consisting of thirty-six dishes, but at that stage I was still unprepared for such a feast!

I particularly liked grilled *bacalhao,* a type of salmon which, I learned, was caught by *Dom* Ricardo's own fishing boats. Someone, possibly Cameron Monroe, had told me that the marquis owned a fleet of such little vessels. It could well have been Cam because, with every minute that passed, I found more evidence to support all that he had tried to tell me.

The *señhora* Salema, Julieta's Aunt Luisa, completely dominated the conversation. She had a habit of putting a question to someone and then answering it herself, or just summarily plunging into another subject before anyone had been given a chance to find a suitable response. This rendered all verbal exchange rather one-sided, which did not upset me. I found it easier not to have to say too much, as it was far more interesting to study the other people at the table. Julieta, who quite naturally enjoyed hearing anecdotes of her childhood, and stories about her parents, was so enthralled that she sometimes forgot to eat.

Dom Ricardo sat on his aunt's right, toying with his food and politely smiling when it was required of him to do so. Whenever he thought it necessary, or the old lady addressed him directly, he would utter a few suitable words and then fall silent again.

It is hardly worthwhile describing the other member of the entourage, Mario. Like any clumsy youth of any nation, he clearly viewed the plate of food in front of him as being of primary interest. Before I had more than tasted mine, his own plate would be polished clean; then he would look around him with obvious boredom, impatiently staring at the ceiling, the pictures on the walls and sometimes—to my discomfort—at me. Once when I looked up and found his almost gaping gaze on me, I looked away very quickly and began to eat as if my life depended upon it.

Isabella was the one in whom I was most interested. She was breathtaking. With dark hair and eyes, an alabaster skin and full red mouth, she was like a perfect Mona Lisa or Madonna, and sadly that perfect beauty was also just as dead as that of a painting.

I was just thinking that I had seldom before encountered such utter 'lifelessness' in anyone, when she suddenly looked up as if she felt my eyes upon her, and favored me with a gentle smile of indescribable loveliness. In that moment, when I looked deeply into those velvety eyes for the first time, it was not difficult to read in them the devastation of sorrow. Whatever her other reasons might have been for marrying Da Silva, she must have loved him deeply. That she missed him was very plain. The grief of his death was clearly discernible in that enchanting, tragic little face; in the listless sagging of her shoulders and the pathetic drooping of her lips.

As I looked from her to her mother, and as my gaze then rested upon the proud, hawk-like face of the Marquis da Monsaraz, I was reminded of what Julieta had said about them, and the way in which she had expressed herself in saying: "Isabella is now a widow and very decidedly back in the marriage market!" now seemed to me to have been rather crude, especially as I had already, earlier that day, come to the conclusion that the exquisite Countess Isabella was on a tight rein, severely held in check by her mother whom she held in awe. Often, when I succeeded in intercepting one of the old lady's critical looks, I almost expected her to say something like: "Isabella, hold your stomach in!" Or, "Isabella sit up straight and keep your shoulders back!"

It was difficult to analyze *Dom* Ricardo's feelings. He seemed to have the power to arouse her occasionally from the pathetic lassitude, he and Isabella seemed to respect and to understand one another very well, and the deep affection between them was almost tangible, but that could easily have been attributed to the fact that they were cousins who had grown up together..

While I was still studying them from where I sat, one of his remarks made her laugh for the first time; and yet, before we had moved our chairs back to rise from the table, I had decided that if the young widow did indeed decide to marry for a second time, and with her cousin, it would mainly be to please her mother. The lovely Isabella with her dainty hands and fine manners, was an ideal candidate to fill the rôle of *Marquise* da Monsaraz, and without a doubt a woman with whom any man could easily fall in love, but it would take her a long time to get over the lamented Count Miguel de Silva!

After such a meal, and with the smell of the sea in my nostrils, it was impossible for me to go and have a siesta indoors with Julieta, Isabella and her grandmother, which provoked the marquis to remark that South African women must have an inexhaustible source of energy, and admirable resistance to heat.

"It is only because we like to make full use of our time, *Señhor Marquis*," I said with some embarrassment. "Until six, short weeks ago, this time of the afternoon was possibly the busiest of my entire day, and I am still not used to such idleness!"

"Oh yes," he remarked, "Julieta mentioned in one of her letters that she worked in the same office as you did ... in the practice of my old friend *Señhor* Cameron Munroe, not so?" For a moment, as I wondered whether the disdain in his voice was a figment of my imagination, I felt myself getting prickly. ... The old hostility was threatening to well up in me once more. Then Julieta's clear young voice was heard from the doorway. "What do you mean, my dear cousin? ... Erin was not simply working in the office; she *was* the office! Just about the entire business! She has long since almost become a better lawyer than Cameron Monroe himself!" Giggling, she turned to address me and I could willingly have strangled her when she came out with: "I swear that the reason why Monroe wanted so badly to marry you, was because he feared that, without you, the practice would collapse!"

"Julieta! You're impossible..." I began, red in the face I'm sure. How on earth had she found that out? But she had already disappeared down the passage to keep her aunt and cousin company during their siesta.

I was truly grateful when the marquis asked me to excuse him for a quarter-hour or so, as he had to put through a phone call to Sintra. He wanted to make sure that certain instructions he had given had been carried out, before he and Julieta departed.

Noël Estardos—the young man with the exemplary manners, who had met us upon our arrival at the harbor the previous day—had meanwhile turned up after visiting his parents in Lisbon, and he and young Mario, having brought out a chessboard, were soon completely engrossed in the game.

For a while I paged disinterestedly through a magazine, but simply could not become absorbed in it. Everything was in Portuguese, which I still had not learned to read, and besides, something was gnawing at my peace of mind

I had a vague idea that it had been wrong of me not to join the ladies. Uncomfortably I wondered if it was considered incorrect for me to have 'chosen' to be the only woman in male company. But then, I tried to console myself by wondering whether, as Julieta, Isabella and the *marquise* probably had many intimate things that they wanted to discuss, I could have forced myself upon them? At length I was just about to give in and go in search of them when another thought arrested me.

Back at the hotel I had seen to it that the marquis was made to understand very clearly that I was not prepared to be subjected to his narrow-minded ideas. With characteristic perversity I was prepared to go to any lengths to flaunt my independence if anything threatened to undermine it. Besides, I owed something to that other South African woman—Julieta's mother—who had reputedly been treated with such disdain just because she was different.

With these thoughts to encourage me, I jumped up out of the deep armchair and, with my chin held high, went out into the garden to walk around in the sunshine.

However, once in the heat, my resolve soon dissipated and I soon fled into the shadow of the great tree under which we had had morning tea. It was there that Ricardo Monsaraz found me.

"The best possible place, *Señorita,*" he said with an unexpected smile which made me actually feel guilty on account of my petulance a few minutes before. "As I said this morning, I'm very much attached to this place and usually come here myself at this time of the day!"

For a while we did not speak. Then he said, slowly as if weighing each word. "I have decided, *Señorita,* that you and Julieta must accompany me when I go to Sintra after the Easter holiday. It is unnecessary and unthinkable for you to remain in that unbearable place any longer. Julieta has been separated from her family for long enough. I think she will enjoy it there and you have already said that you very much want to see more of the country. In Sintra you will be able to see more of the genuine Portuguese way of life than is possible in the city!"

"It is very good of you, *Señhor* ..." I began, uncertain as to how to continue. "And it would make Julieta very happy, that I know. Naturally it would make me happy too to know that her family welcomed her with open arms. I'm very much attached to her and often pitied her loneliness in Johannesburg."

"She's very fortunate to have such a loyal friend as you are *Señorita*. It is immediately possible to see how much she values your friendship... how she admires you. Naturally, although we are related, there will be many days when she will feel strange and confused. She has been gone from this country and away from us for too long. Later I shall see to it that her cousin, the Countess Isabella, takes her around as much as possible, but in the beginning I think she will be happier if you, the one person she knows well, and truly loves, is close by. If you would decide to forget the traveling around for a while, and make your home with us, I would greatly appreciate it...

"I should particularly appreciate it if, during the next few days, you would accompany me when I take Julieta to do some shopping. I would very much like to take her to a few of the fashionable boutiques and give her an opportunity to acquire some of the little trinkets and other odds and ends for which her heart has probably longed since the death of her parents."

"That is very good of you, *Señhor*," I repeated, still confused, and then I felt embarrassed because I could think of no other suitable rejoinder except to add: "Julieta has excellent taste and can be very sensible about things like that. Nevertheless, if you think that my presence and encouragement can in any way contribute to the success of the expedition, I would very much enjoy accompanying you. ... The invitation to accompany you to Sintra I also accept with the greatest pleasure!"

That night I could happily write to both the Meirings and Cameron: "Wonderful news! Julieta's days of uncertainty are assuredly behind her. She has passed all tests with flying colors. I left her alone with *Dom* Ricardo for a while and her own captivating personality won him over completely; thus achieving far more than ten years of testimonials could have done.

"He, *Dom* Ricardo, announced this afternoon that she would be accompanying him, and living in the *palacio* when he returns to Sintra for the remainder of holidays. On his invitation I am to accompany them.

"From tomorrow onwards, during the few days that still remain before Good Friday, we are to take Julieta on a shopping spree. A gesture of good faith on the part of the marquis.

"I really don't know why we were concerned for even a single moment. It was not even really necessary for me to have come, because I find that I am the one who has to mind my p's and in q's, and not she!

"Surroundings are very important, but blood is thicker than water. Among her family she is the perfect little *señorita* ... charming, dignified and completely at home. They have taken her to their hearts without reservation; as a matter of fact the awe-inspiring Ricardo is quite besotted with her.

"I only hope that Carlos—whose acquaintance we made yesterday—will fare equally well in the long run. From what he confided to me yesterday the future does not look too rosy for him at the moment because *Dom* Ricardo is a difficult man, completely intractable, and Carlos—probably as his father had been before him—is a born rebel!"

Carlos! The mere mention of him made me think again about the singular young man. Twice in little more than twenty-four hours, he was almost the cause of unpleasantness. Of course I did not relate this to Cameron or Angela, but I sat pondering the situation for a long time, and when I resumed my letter-writing, I was almost too angry to be able to concentrate.

Before *Dom* Ricardo had brought us home, we had visited the casino as I'd been hoping that we might do. After that, after sunset we walked along the beach and had tea—or actually coffee. Our host had beach chairs brought for us. Isabella and her mother had sat down first and while we waited for the rest of the chairs, Julieta and I threw ourselves down on the sand, loving it.

"It is very pleasant here," I heard the señora Salema say. "It does one good sometimes to see the family gathered together as a whole. ... Just a pity that Carlos is not also here. Julieta could have come to know him today, as well."

She turned slightly to be able to see us better and unexpectedly she addressed me.

"I have another nephew whose acquaintance you must make, *Señorita* March. The young man must still be tamed somewhat, but I think that you would find him quite pleasant."

"I made his acquaintance yesterday, *Señora*" I was able to tell her. "And I fully expected him to be here."

"*Señorita March* is a dedicated defendant of downtrodden young men," Ricardo da Monsaraz observed with a cynical amusement.. "I discovered that yesterday, to my sorrow. She is going to be a cause of great complexity for me if she approves of everything that Carlos does!" Immediately he set my blood boiling all over again. Forgotten were my repeated resolutions to be friendly towards him. I cannot abide bossy people! And why did everyone always have to go off about Carlos when the young man was not present to defend himself? They were all so ready to regard his youth and way of life as almost criminal!

"Carlos and I have a great deal in common," was my response ...meant for *Dom* Ricardo. "I also enjoy defying convention!"

Only when I slid in between the cool sheets that night and relived the day did I fully begin to appreciate the colossal extent of Ricardo' da Monsaraz' self-assurance. He had not actually invited me to be his guest at the *palacio*. On the contrary. *"I have decided ..."* he had said. *He* had decided and that was that! Truly the man was impossible!

I sighed with sheer exasperation; at the same time aware that my face was burning.

'So what did *you* do, my tender little lamb?' I demanded sarcastically of myself. ... "Sat there meekly," I recalled furiously, and then sweetly replied: "It is very kind of you, *Señhor Marqui*s!"

Chapter Six

Despite my solemn determination never ever again to allow my reserve to waver in the company of the marquis, I thoroughly enjoyed the week before we left Sintra. Reluctantly or not, I simply found myself thawing every time he elected to exert that devastating charm.

There were a few occasions on which I 'bared my teeth' as was the case on the morning he sent me back to the house to fetch a hat or a sunshade, and on the afternoon when he forbade me to go outside after lunch unless I'd had a rest. I cannot be honest without confessing that he won the argument on every occasion.

In my heart I knew that I had, in the first place, purposely (and very soon to my regret) left the hat indoors just to infuriate him. The urge to go to the shops again after I had already had ample time to buy all I wanted, earlier that morning, had only been precipitated by a desire to spite him. ... To console myself when I had once again suffered a defeat. ... Then later, as would usually be the case, I would have to admit to myself that it had purely been kindness and concern that had prompted his conduct. Nevertheless, in the face of that I would, while gnashing my teeth, wonder why he had to be so domineering. There was ever that perversity in myself that would never permit anyone to dominate me.

Every morning the magnificent La Gonda would draw up at the front door and so would begin another day of trivial but exhilarating activity. We would generally go to some exclusive boutique upon which we had had already settled the day before, and then, as usual, the entire staff would appear to be at the disposal of *Dom* Ricardo and his guests. To both Julieta and me it was an experience and a rare privilege to shop in such circumstances. There we would linger until about eleven o'clock and then enjoy refreshments in some place of interest before taking a tour through it. Indeed a rare privilege to do so in the company of a man whose family had probably been associated with it in some way or another since the time of its establishment.

Because there were many business affairs which, of course, also demanded his attention he usually took us home before three o'clock, and then we would happily spend the afternoons, breathless as Julieta opened the parcels with trembling fingers, and had a good look at the wonderful things that had been selected that morning, to be added to her fast-growing collection of treasures.

"Oh, Erin," she would frequently cry out ecstatically as she paraded in front of the mirror in another of the breathtaking garments for which she was indebted to her generous cousin. "Isn't Ricardo wonderful? I feel like a fairy princess! I'm so scared that this is all a dream from which I might awake too soon!"

I shared her delight, inevitably with misty eyes, and I had no option but to admit that, as far as she was concerned, the marquis certainly deserved those accolades..

To my acute embarrassment I was never forgotten, either. Even if it only happened to be a dainty lace handkerchief, a book I had wanted for many years, or a posy of delicate white violets—I was *obliged* to choose something for myself!

I did demur—once—but that was the last time...

"I find your fierce independence admirable, *Señorita* Erin," was his reaction. "My experience of young women, which I owe solely to my nieces and the daughters of friends, had led me to believe that to persuade innocent men folk to buy all the trinkets and ornamentations that are so dear to their little hearts is their main object in life. Nevertheless, to be a gracious recipient is also a beautiful and gracious art which is worthy of cultivation, and one which one should practice when one has the privilege and the opportunity presents itself."

Well, how was I to respond to that? And that is how I came to acquire the gorgeous black *mantilla*, the lace headdress which has so often been admired ever since it came into my possession. That was the day he told us about the olive festival.

In the store *Dom* Ricardo insisted that I try on the *mantilla*.

"Come on, Erin!" Julieta cried enthusiastically. "How can you be sure whether or not you like it, unless you do?"

She and the stout, middle-aged assistant together, helped me to put it on, and then went back to where the man stood in order to get a better view from there.

I turned self-consciously to display the effect, and unexpectedly looked up directly into the dark, smoldering eyes of Ricardo da Monsaraz. Before I could look away from that intense gaze, I felt the hot blood rise to my face.

"Enchanting!" was his observation. "That is truly one of the loveliest fashions ever to come from Spain.—*Señorita* Erin, permit me to assure you that no Spanish *señorita* ever looked more charming in one!"

"Thank you, Ricardo," I managed to smile bashfully, still painfully aware of my burning cheeks. "Thank you for both a charming gift and a charming compliment!"

"No, indeed," declared the assistant in her businesslike way. "It suits you admirably." She turned roguishly to *Dom* Ricardo. "In my opinion black lace is manufactured specifically to adorn such blonde hair." While he studied me amusedly as though wishing to make sure that that was truly the case, I felt myself once more blushing like a schoolgirl.

"What a pity that it is too late for the carnival now. Such a mantle would have been ideal to wear to something like that."

"On, no!" Julieta cried out disappointedly. "Are we really too late for it, Ricardo?"

"I'm afraid you are, *Menina* (little girl.) Don't you remember? The big carnival always takes place on the Sunday before Ash Wednesday." He broke off and suddenly smiled indulgently. "But wait! I had almost forgotten! I know of something that will please you two. ... Wait until we get to the café and then I'll tell you. At first I was not too eager to go, but *Señorita* Erin must be given an opportunity to do justice to that black lace—or what do you say?"

Julieta pleaded in vain. Laughingly he would only repeat that she would have to be patient. In this mood the marquis became youthful and unbelievably charming. I would have found him quite lovable, if that were possible.

Later he informed us that *Dom* Gil, Isabella's father had telephoned to ask if he would consider postponing our departure for Sintra, for a day or two, so that we could attend the olive festival at their *quinta*. The harvest had already been brought in, but as a celebration of that nature could not take place during Lent, it would be held on Easter Monday.

"You will certainly enjoy it," the marquis told us. "As with the carnival, fun and music will be the order of the day. Everyone casts inhibitions aside. All the farmers in the vicinity, everyone who is employed on *Tia* Luisa's estate, all the neighbors and their families. They'll all be there! It will, however, perhaps be advisable to make sure that everyone has a partner for the evening. ... Julieta, Noël Estardos has already requested that he might be permitted to accompany you if we do decide to go. ... Then, of course, there are Isabella and young Mario, and, in the circumstances, it would perhaps be better for her to attend with her brother." He regarded me thoughtfully. "You, *Señorita* Erin will come with me, and then, together with *Dom* Gil and Tia Luisa we'd be a nice, equal number."

"Thank you, *Señhor*, came my submissive rejoinder, which astounded me. "I look forward to it!"

When we temporarily returned to our hotel in Lisbon, it was only natural after what had been such eventful and pleasure-filled days and nights, that we should now find the evenings dull and boring by contrast. It was thus only natural, I tried to convince myself, that I should be counting the days until we left to go to the festival. On many occasions I wondered how Ricardo da Monsaraz spent his evenings. ... Did he like going to the theater? And with whom?

Isabella and her mother had already returned to the farm, or *quinta*, as it was known, three days before that.

Often in my imagination I could see the marquis in faultless evening dress, the dark, proud face ennobled by the starched white shirt and black bow tie, and then I always pictured him in the company of a suitable companion. ... Dark, shining hair and creamy skin; white shoulders exposed above the perfect sheath of an evening gown ... priceless pearls, expensive perfume and glittering jewels. I could never complete the dream, however, because the woman's face would always evade me.

Sometimes, with greater effort, I could picture him alone in his beautiful garden, or in armchair with a favorite book in his hand. He and Noël, the secretary, facing each other across a chessboard. ... Don Ricardo wandering alone along the moonlit Estoril beach. For some inexplicable reason this last thought was more pleasant to me than the others.

As I have said, the evenings were lonely for us. Usually we sat and read for a while or would write letters before going to bed early, because it was apparently unthinkable that we would venture outside after sunset without a man to accompany us. It was therefore almost a relief when Carlos turned up unexpectedly on the Wednesday evening before Good Friday. His university was, of course, closed for a few days, and he had thus decided to come and spend his short leave with us in Lisbon. Acting on Julieta's advice he went to consult the management and was fortunate enough to find a room just one floor above ours.

It was already too late to plan for visits to any of the places of interest, and, in any case, it was rather nice just to sit and chat. Usually at about 8:45 we would walk across to the park opposite the hotel where, for a while, we would listen to an orchestra. On the first evening, after ordering ice cold lime juice for us, Carlos dug a letter from his pocket.

"It's from my mum," he explained, "and I really cannot decide what to do." He frowned and scratched his head concernedly.

"Why?" Julia wanted to know. "Is something wrong?" I also looked questioningly at him.

"Wait," he said, unfolding the letter. "I'll read it to you."

Way back, at our first meeting on the afternoon of our arrival in the city, he had already given me to understand that his mother was not at all happy about his decision to come to Portugal. She was of the opinion that he had, so far, managed quite well enough at home without any assistance from his father's family, and that he should continue to carry on as he had been accustomed to doing. A moment later he brought to light a wrinkled envelope, and after what I heard from Cameron concerning the old *marquise's* treatment of her two daughters in-law I could not say that I blamed Carlos's mother for what she had written.

What he now proceeded to read to us was thus only a confirmation of what was already known to me. Mrs. Da Monsaraz was clearly lonely without her son and looked forward impatiently to the day when he would relinquish all the 'ridiculous dreams of a fortune,'—as she put it—and come back home to Britain.

"Sometimes I really do feel like going back home," he confided desperately after he had replaced the letter safely back in its envelope. "I'm also beginning to think that I am just wasting my time!" The very next moment the sunny grin that I found so appealing was back, and he shrugged his shoulders. "Don't mind me! I am talking absolute nonsense! *Of course* I am going to stick it out. Ricardo is actually not such a bad sort. Perhaps something will yet come over him, and make the wait worthwhile."

"I think I can appreciate your mother's point of view," I responded thoughtfully. "As you have made clear, she is a proud woman and it must grieve her to have her son also waiting for a sign of approval; no matter how trivial it might be..."

"Yes, but don't you understand, Erin, that is precisely *why*! For the very reason that my grandmother caused her so much grief, I must get a share of that estate—no matter how small—and I shall see to it that my mother is the one who benefits from it!"

"I thought you wanted the money to further your studies?" Julieta asked, rather than stated, which annoyed me. She could not be permitted to become smug because Ricardo overwhelmed *her* with so many gestures of his approval.

The young man's face was a shade paler and very solemn as he leant forward, and his reply was barely audible.

"My mother will not be able to remain independent forever," he told us fiercely. "What I spend on my studies is an investment in her future. The better my qualifications the more I can do for her some day when she will most need me to do so. As things are, she would never touch a penny of Grandmother's money, but when the dividends start arriving indirectly through me, she will be proud to receive them!"

In my estimation, at any rate, he had risen considerably!

Back at the hotel we kept to the subject of the olive festival to which both Julieta and I looked forward eagerly.

When Ricardo ascended the broad staircase of the hotel next morning and found Carlos there with us, I knew at once that the blessed peace of the past few days had been irretrievably shattered. The smile that had brightened those aquiline features and had so unbelievably changed them, had disappeared behind an impenetrable mask of cool, critical hauteur. His face was a picture of indifference when he asked whether we were ready to depart. He did not invite Carlos to accompany us, and that morning's excursion was far from a success.

Back at the hotel my, by now already low spirits, were soon to sink even further when Carlos came to meet us and informed us that he had been in touch with *Tia* Luisa.

"She has invited me to the festival, as well," he told us enthusiastically, "and has suggested that you might be kind enough to make room for me in your car, Ricardo."

For the first time I knew Ricardo to be openly ungracious. "There are already four of us..."he began discouragingly.

"Oh, let him come, Ricardo," Julieta interrupted. "I know that Erin will also be pleased.!"

"If there is not enough room," Carlos replied good-naturedly—for which I could willingly have murdered him—"you can always sit on my lap, Erin!"

Ricardo stiffened but not even a flicker of his eyelids betrayed what he was thinking.

"Well then," he said expressionlessly, "I shall pick the three of you up before nine o'clock on Monday morning. "Mario will just have to be the odd-man out, but I doubt if he will be without a partner for too long!"

With that he greeted us very politely and when the distinctive car had passed by the big glass doors a few minutes later I remained standing there, wondering why I suddenly felt so depressed. It was not difficult to guess what he had meant by that last remark. Carlos would, of course, now be my companion and he, Ricardo, would be taking the beautiful Isabella to the celebrations!

Suddenly I no longer looked forward so much to the celebrations on the *quinta.* Doubt assailed me. The strain of a whole day and night among strangers might be too exacting. If I had to pay attention all the time, to what I said and did, it might be very difficult to behave normally. In that atmosphere I could well understand how Carlos might feel.

As was generally the case when they got together, Julieta and Carlos spent the time now teasing one another in a half-playful, half-serious manner. Unnoticed I turned and went to our bedroom to finish that letter I had started to write to Cameron two nights before.

That I had begun it in a particularly upbeat frame of mind, was easy to read between the lines That morning Ricardo had bought the *mantilla* for me and I had eagerly described every detail of it to Cam.

"Ricardo is really not as awe-inspiring when one gets to know him, you know. He is a tremendous guide—probably because all the places of interest are known so well to him—and he is able to tell one the history of every edifice, monument and building.

"I did tell you in my previous letter that he was planning to take Julieta to all the leading shops. Well now she says she feels like Cinderella, herself!

"This morning he bought me the loveliest present—a black, lace mantilla, which I plan to wear to the olive festival which is to take place at Dom Gil and the señhora Salema's quinta."

After that I chewed the end of my pen for at least twenty minutes, agonizing about how to continue. Cameron was so insightful and knew me so well. Suddenly I missed him intensely. If only there could have been hope of his also being at the *quinta,* there would have been nothing to dread because he was always able to instill such abundant confidence in me. It astonished me to perceive how much I had depended on him over the years and I reluctantly had to admit to myself that he had spoilt me outrageously. With Cam I was only required to be myself. ... It had never been necessary to put myself out to be particularly elegant or endearing.

"April 15," I began at last, and wrote briefly:

"Have been trying for two days to finish this note. Sorry not to have posted it sooner.

"Carlos is here and is also going south with us to the quinta. Only too relieved that it is not necessary for me to have to go to the feast with the inflexible Dom Ricardo.

"In any case I can't say that I am looking forward unduly to attending the affair. It can be uncomfortable to be the only 'foreigner' among so many strangers.

"Will write again when we get to the palacio next week.

"As always,

"Erin"

Chapter Seven

I don't know why I was ever so apprehensive. ... Of course I had forgotten the famed Portuguese hospitality.

Tia Luisa, as our hostess, was more than hospitable; she was concern and caring personified. Isabella seemed genuinely glad to see us (life must often have been very lonely for her) and even Mario managed to favor me with a shy smile.

But is was *Dom* Gil who made me feel at home as I had never completely been since my last glimpse of Table Mountain. The short, gentle little man with the deep brown eyes was like a friendly brown squirrel. The way he would look at one piercingly with his head slightly tilted to one side, only served to intensify this impression. Grey hair and a small, silver-flecked beard reminded me of my favorite uncle—one of my mother's brothers.

Whenever Tia Luisa's voice rose to become a tad more shrill than usual, he would smile encouragingly and look at us apologetically as though to say: "Don't worry! Don't be alarmed! She is not as cross as she seems!"—No wonder Ricardo and his uncle were clearly so fond of each other.

The elderly nobleman spoke little, but when he did, it was always worthwhile to listen to him; he soon revealed himself to be an avid reader whose general knowledge was amazing.

He asked after Cameron, about whom he had heard a great deal, and I told him that I regretted the fact that they had not been able to meet during Cam's visit to Portugal. Because they seemed to me to have so much in common, they would have enjoyed each other's company.

One thing the old man said to me when we found ourselves alone before lunch, particularly assured him of my permanent regard.

"I like South African women, "he said with an impish smile. "They're full of fire! Did you know that Julieta's mother was Afrikaans?—beautiful woman, and very congenial. ... Blonde, like you, *Señorita*—and nobody was ever allowed to 'sit on her head,' as the saying goes. Courage of her own convictions!"

Something in his expression caused me to shriek with mirth. Probably the mischievous wink. He joined in the laughter; albeit more restrainedly, and that is how Ricardo found us when the gong summoned us inside. After lunch and during the unavoidable *siesta,* Isabella and I chose to remain outdoors and we went to sit under a giant magnolia tree.

"Oh, it's delightful out here," I sighed contentedly and, with my hands under my head, stretched out, full-length, in the deck chair "I love country life. Sometimes I wonder why I wasted all those years before my parents died, in the city, and did not rather go home!"

"That is good, "she said in her soft voice, "because then you are going to enjoy Sintra. Ricardo's farm is not very different from this, except that the lands are not quite as extensive and he farms more with livestock than crops."

"At the *palacio*? I asked, surprised. "Is there a farm, as well?"

"Certainly there is. It is virtually also a *quinta*. We more often make mention of the *'palacio,'* for the house is so magnificent, and it is the seat of the Da Monsaraz family."

We sat there companionably for quite a while, sometimes chatting and remaining wrapped in thought at others. Once, when I heard her sigh deeply, I turned involuntarily to look at her, and to study her anew. I was at least two years older than she was, and yet, in her pitiful earnestness and seeing the solemnity in those big, expressive eyes, she made me feel years younger.

Finally we rose to go indoors; she to assist her mother with preparations for coffee and I to find Juliet so that we could have a final discussion about our clothes for the evening. Thus far the day had passed very pleasantly and I could find no cause for the niggling feeling of melancholy that lurked in the dark corners of my subconscious to disrupt my peace of mind—until shortly before seven o'clock I joined the others, including Carlos, who awaited me, together with the old folks. Julieta and Noël, reprimanded me good-naturedly for my tardiness before adding reproachfully: "Ricardo and Isabella went on ahead of us about five minutes ago."

I had taken particular care with my appearance that evening. I wore my wide, black cotton skirt with the low-necked white, silk blouse such as the peasant girls wore, and it went every bit as well with it as I had hoped. The obviously genuine admiration expressed by my companions, when I joined them, should have been more then gratifying, but for some reason I no longer derived any satisfaction form the knowledge that I looked nice.

"Quite perfect!" called out the gallant *Dom* Gil when he saw me. "But one important detail is missing." With that, standing on tiptoe to reach it, he plucked a large magnolia flower which he gallantly fastened in my hair, just above my left ear. Julieta wore a similar bloom in hers.

"Yes, truly," she agreed. "That makes all the difference. That white flower is gorgeous against the background of the black lace!"

"Breathtaking, *Minja señorita,*" said Noël Estardos, to my surprise, and then, to add to my acute embarrassment, he favored me with a courtly bow.

I knew that I was blushing when I thanked them, but the smile that I feigned for their gratification required no small effort because I was immediately reminded of what Carlos had said shortly before that, and which meant that that I was no longer to be the lucky girl that Ricardo da Monsaraz would have at his side all evening! Isabella was now to have that privilege!

It was then that, like a flash of blinding lightning, much became clear to me with a suddenness that made me dizzy.

I was in love with Ricardo da Monsaraz!

Without any doubt whatsoever I could now find a reason for all the clashing emotions that had been assailing me recently. It was for him, and for him alone that I had dressed so carefully that evening.

Deeply unhappy I wondered how I was to get through the evening; how I should conduct myself so that no one would guess. It took a great deal to converse naturally so that Julieta and the rest would not find my behavior peculiar.

Carlos and his uncle each carried a lantern to light the way through the undergrowth for us. With every step the sound of laughter amid the merrymaking became more audible. At length we came to an open space where the tables had already been laid out in readiness for our arrival. Overhanging branches were festooned with dozens of lanterns which, as they shone through the trees, wove interesting patterns on the ground below and lent a romantic unreality to the entire surrounding area.

The meal consisting of an overwhelming selection of dishes seemed interminable that night. There were numerous *hors d'oevres*, countless fish dishes and a selection of more than a dozen kinds of meat, among which the most popular proved to be venison and partridge, but I could only swallow with difficulty. Most of the time I was too busy trying to tear my eyes away from the opposite end of the table, where Ricardo was engaged in animated conversation with the wife of one of *Dom* Gil's neighbors.

On his right, quiet and beautiful as ever, sat Isabella. Now and then he would bend over as though to inquire after her wellbeing. When I caught her once, just as she looked up into his dark, proud face, I almost hated her for being so lovely. Any woman who could sit so passively beside him, untouched by the man's sheer magnetism, could not be normal, I thought once.

Dom Gil's household, as well as that of his honored guests, sat together at one, long table. Their servants and those of the other farmer who were present, chose to stand, 'buffet-fashion,' with a chicken leg or a cold potato in his or her hand—as we might have done at a picnic back home. The lights swayed in the gentle evening breeze and in the background I could hear the strumming of guitars, accompanied by an accordion and two violins.

"I'm sure I am the *only* one here who is feeling so wretched," I sat thinking despairingly.

Then, unexpectedly the feasting was forsaken as the dancing began.

The orchestra suddenly switched to music of a different kind, and as if that were a signal, the young men hastily began to search for their partners. *Dom* Gil offered his arm to *Tia* Luisa and went ahead with her to a low stage that had been erected to one side; some of the other, elderly people, following their example. As soon as Ricardo rose to lead Isabella in that direction, Noël gestured to Carlos that he should also bring me there.

Chairs had been provided so that those who did not wish to dance would be able to have a good view of those who did, which was fortunate. Most of the dances were completely unknown to me but I enjoyed being a spectator and enthusiastically clapped my hands in time to the rhythm. Ricardo once led his aunt onto the floor for a stately waltz, and later I danced both a tango and a waltz with Carlos.

Eventually, however, most people did a sort of folk dance that did not seem so complicated to me. It was more like prancing around wildly in a polka than anything else and to my astonishment many of the older people also cavorted with much exuberance. Everyone who participated did so amid much laughter and with obvious enjoyment.

Carlos, watched the spectacle intently for some moments; then abruptly grabbed me by the arm. "That looks so easy. Why don't we also give it a go, Erin?" At which Ricardo apologized to Isabella and took Julieta instead.

It was the sort of dance in which partners separated after each round. Everyone then moved in opposite directions; the men to the right and the ladies to the left. Each time the music stopped, someone at the end of the line would be without a partner, leaving those who were left behind on the dance floor to change partners. The rest would then have to go and wait against a tree trunk with his or her arms folded behind their backs.

I was the third one to drop out. Self-conscious as any other female would probably have been, when I went over to lean against a tree with my hands behind my back I kept looking down at my feet, and when I did look up it was to find Ricardo beside me.

Temporarily, after all the effort and unfamiliar exercise which so wild a dance had exacted, I found that a heavy weight had been lifted from my heart. I stood panting and (I was sure) with glowing cheeks.

"Did you have to drop out, too, *Senhor?*" I laughed breathlessly.

He smiled affirmatively and the blood throbbed loudly in my ears. I was painfully aware of his nearness.

"Are you enjoying yourself, *Pequena*? (Little one)" he asked, also a little short of breath.

"Oh, yes, *Senhor* ...thank you very much!"

"The black lace has obviously exceeded all expectations! I very much like the white flower, and the scent of it is glorious even from a distance!" To my consternation he bent forward to smell it close up.

"*Dom* Gil insisted upon it," I explained, hastily, and drew back because it unnerved me to have his face so close to mine. "He picked it for me, himself, and put it in my hair."

"It is obvious that he likes you, Erin, and I have always regarded him as one who really knows human kind. He is a consummate judge of character."

The next dance had begun without my being aware of it. I was at a loss as to how to respond to him and could only smile with embarrassment while wondering how this man always managed to make me feel so clumsy and inexperienced. With Cameron Monroe I had never been at a loss for words. At the same time, while not really 'seeing' them, I had noticed that Carlos was dancing with Julieta, and abstractedly realized that Noël, who now sat alone on the stage, did not seem to be too happy about it.

I must have looked at Julieta and her partner for longer than I realized, and Ricardo must have found his own explanation for my silence, because he astounded me by suddenly grabbing me quite roughly by the arm, making me turn around so that I looked fully in his face.

"Why do you squander your tears and hidden feelings on such a shallow character, Erin?" he demanded passionately; his teeth clenched and his voice hardly above a hiss. "Carlos is far too shallow ever to make you happy. He is the kind of man who necessarily has to lean on a woman…"

"*Señhor!*" I gasped; startled but nevertheless emboldened by sheer rage. "Now you are overstepping the mark! I waste my feelings on no one, much less am I jealous of Carlos as you so clearly seem to think! … Furthermore you do him a great disservice when you describe him as being shallow."

"I beg your pardon, *Señorita*," he responded stiffly, instantly the dignified marquis once more. His eyes could have been compared with coals of fire. "But your fervent defense of the man is precisely what I would have expected. Women are so easily drawn to helpless men!"

My hands shook uncontrollably and I could barely rely on my voice. I knew that tears were very close. But this bickering about Carlos, the hints and the caustic remarks, had now gone on for long enough. A stop had to be put to this once and for all.

I chose my words very carefully. "*Señhor*, I defend Carlos purely because I cannot bear injustice."

"So you consider me unfair and unjust?"

"I think that you're prejudiced and that injustice may spring from that. Carlos now has to be punished because, according to your standards, his father sinned!"

"Not according to *my* standards.—According to those set by my grandmother for whom I cherished the greatest respect, and for whose memory I still do. A man has no right to allow his heart to overrule duty. Carlos's father was already engaged to the daughter of one of the greatest friends of our family!"

"That has nothing to do with this subject, but of course I am one of those old-fashioned, sentimental people who believe that love is the most important of all. The question under discussion is whether you are prejudiced or not, and you have now affirmed that yourself..." I was so eager for the subject to be closed that I now began to plead in earnest. ... "Don't you, yourself, think that you're being a little unjust where the young man is concerned? Have you any idea ... have you ever tried to understand ... how unpleasant Carlos must find his current position? I have —and I assure you that I pity him from the bottom of my heart. ... How would you like to be regarded like a sheep at an auction? Everybody prodding you ... examining your teeth ... pulling your ears until it hurts ... before they can finally decide whether or not they want to buy you. ... and then still argue about the price! Carlos has more pride than you think, *Senhor*, and it must truly be unbearable for him at times!"

Whether it was my outrageous analogy or not, I do not know, but Ricardo suddenly burst out laughing. He threw his head back and roared so delightedly that people turned around to look at us, just to see what could be so funny.

"Truly, Erin, p*equena*," he spluttered while I faced him uncertainly, "Julieta was right. You're not just a good lawyer You are a first-class advocate to boot!"

That was when he took my hand and led me to a seat to discuss the matter further. He went to fetch each of us a drink and, temporarily oblivious of all the people around us, we sat talking earnestly but in a friendly manner for certainly more than half-an-hour. A thought that instantly went through my head was that, for the first time, Carlos had caused something besides unpleasantness between us. The happiness that radiated from my face, must have been clearly visible to everybody, but I did not care. It was just so wonderful that we were once more on a friendly footing.

I told him all I knew. How unhappy Carlos's mother was alone in Scotland; why Carlos endured the humiliation of his present position, and what he was planning to do with his share of the *Marquise's* bequest in the event that he received it. And Ricardo then talked to me about his grandmother, confiding his tremendous love and respect for her, and candidly explaining to me how difficult it was for him to carry out her wishes as meticulously as she expected him to.

"Now you see, Little One, it's not just a question of whether I like Carlos or not. I have a tremendous responsibility. The main condition of Grandmother's will is that Carlos and Julieta must be able to satisfy me that they will conduct themselves at all times in a respectful and conservative manner, according to the standards of our family.

"My grandmother loved everything for which her family stood, *Pequena,* and not just the money or the title. I had already incurred her disapproval by becoming the first member of her family to become involved in commercial affairs, and now I must at least carry out my promise devotedly by being faithful to her other wishes." With a deep sigh he turned and, palms upturned in a gesture of resignation, regarded me almost beseechingly. "Now that you know my side of the story, please tell me what it is that you want me to do!"

I weighed my response seriously for a moment before, amazed at my own temerity, I said, "Well then, I shall tell you. ... First you must be prepared to give him a chance. How can you ever hope to know what he is really like when you see him so seldom? Secondly, why not for just a little while, try not to provoke him to become defensive, and then you will see how courteous, careful and caring he can be. You see, *Dom Ricardo*"—and it cost me a great deal to have to confess this to him—"I know how he is, because I'm like that myself. Very perverse! Every time you try to control us, you make our hair stand on end, and what is the result?

We go to the utmost in the opposite direction, just to shock you!"

"I see!" he said with a crooked smile. "I see!"

The orchestra leader, violin under his chin, was now busy wandering around amongst the people, asking for requests just as I'd often seen in movies, and when I happened to look up, he took it for granted that I was summoning him, and eagerly came hurrying forward.

"What shall it be, *Señorita*? You only have to name it. ... A tango? A samba? ... Love song?. Pedro is ready to play it for you!" I could not look at Ricardo but answered without hesitation: *April in Portugal*, please Pedro. **Coimbra!***"

Ricardo extended his hand.

"Come, let us dance, *Pequena*, because the party is coming to an end and I must return to Isabella!"

※

On the following afternoon, while Julieta and I were in the hotel closing our suitcases before Ricardo came to fetch us, Carlos knocked at the door, having come to take leave of us.

"What do you think, darlings, the dragon has relented! Ricardo has invited me to spend every free weekend I am granted, at the *palacio*! Did I not predict that something would still happen, some day to soften his heart?"

He looked so excited that I could hardly bear to dampen his enthusiasm but an attitude like that could be risky and, besides that, I did not like it very much.

"Look here, Carlos, if *Dom* Ricardo has invited you he has done so as a gesture of kindness and friendship and is one you cannot belittle! It must have taken a man of his nature and character a great deal to take the first step and I hope with all my heart that you will not disappoint him. Never forget that he has been burdened with a great responsibility. That it cannot be easy to carry out his grandmother's wishes faithfully. Please be a bit decent to him now, in return!" I pleaded. "Don't put yourself out to challenge him again!"

"**What**!" Carlos exclaimed incredulously; one eyebrow arched questioningly as he addressed his young cousin—who shrugged her shoulders with exaggerated dismay. "And now who's talking? Seems to me the same 'something, that 'softened *his* heart' has gone to work on *hers*!"

Chapter Eight

I arrived at the *palacio* to find a letter from Cameron waiting for me, and when Ricardo's housekeeper took me to my bedroom a while later, I was touched to see a lovely bouquet of roses from him. "To welcome you and make you feel at home in a strange place!"

There was a lump in my throat as I read his card which he must have cabled to have it there in time, but that was how I had always known him to be. Few men concern themselves with the small things that women find so important.

His letter was not quite as comforting. It had been written in response to the one I had dashed off on the night we arrived back at the hotel from Estoril, and it came as a warning that it was dangerous to allow Julieta's expectations to rise too high. "Your conclusion that all is now rosy seems to me to be somewhat premature Erin," is how he put it, "and you have had enough experience of such matters to know by now that nothing is legal until one has it in black and white."

At that moment I was, however, far too taken up with the beautiful house and the splendid things housed in it to take much notice of Cam's pessimism. Only vaguely was I aware that it gratified me to read, at the end of his note, that he would never forget me and that he should not be blamed if he murdered Suzanne Tredoux someday. "Sometimes she makes me so angry that I could throttle her! Oh Erin, Erin, how dreadfully you spoilt me!" ... And only two days before that I had realized, for the first time, *how much he had spoilt me!"*

But these things were of minor importance. I had heard so much about the *palacio* that in time it had become a sort of legend to me. To see it for myself was extremely thrilling— like something out of a fairytale, heard as a child— and now in some amazing way become a reality.

During the first week of our sojourn there, Julieta and I had felt like two princesses, staying in bed till goodness knows what hour every morning. We were, in fact, even served breakfast in bed. (Delicious bread rolls which the cook had only just taken out of the oven, and homemade butter with honey that brought the aroma of apple blossoms with it.)

Ricardo, who generally left home early to go to Sintra, always returned before lunch, and usually there would be guests who spent the afternoons and sometimes stayed on until at least ten o'clock at night. There was a splendid grand piano in the spacious salon, so there was never a lack of good music. It seemed to me that it was expected of every young Portuguese lady that she should learn to play and sing. We seldom if ever saw Ricardo alone.

But on the Saturday morning I announced that my laziness had come to an end. From then on, I told Ricardo and Julieta, I was determined to get outside while the dew was still on the ground. I very much wanted to explore the property before the worst heat of the day and Ricardo spontaneously inquired as to whether we liked riding horses. It appeared that it was his habit to go riding in the mornings, before breakfast. Julieta was quick to admit that she was terrified of horses, and besides, she still enjoyed the luxury of sleeping late in the mornings, but I was happily able to state that I had spent hours in the saddle on my father's farm.

"When I get home this afternoon I'm going to see if I can borrow a pair of riding breeches for you from someone, Erin, until we can go and buy some for you," he said when I told him that. "And tomorrow morning I'm going to choose a mount for you!"

The days that followed were amongst the most delightful I had ever spent. Of course I was always somewhat tense in Ricardo's presence because my greatest fear was that some day I would betray how I felt about him, but his conduct was completely natural. While I had the sweet joy that his nearness afforded I eagerly grasped the privilege with both hands.

The world was indescribably beautiful early in the morning, with the glistening dewdrops still on the grass, small streams of water sparkling in the rising sun, the blood singing in my veins because I could once more feel a sturdy horse, under me and because, at this time of the day, Ricardo and I could have been the only people on earth for an hour or so.

How my father would have enjoyed the opportunity to choose a mount for himself from stables like Ricardo's!

One morning when he, Ricardo, and I sat alone at the breakfast table, he reminded me of the visit to the tile factory, which we had discussed that day in Estoril.

"Still interested in going, *Pequena*?"

"Oh yes! I would really like to, thank you. Shall I go and tell Julieta about it?"

"Yes, please. In that case it might be a good plan to get her out from between her sheets a little earlier, because I need to get to the factory in time to see the manager before he goes to Sintra to do the banking."

On our way through the entrance hall, I found two letters; one from Cam for me, and one with a Lisbon stamp on it for Julieta. I took hers to her bedroom with me.

She stretched out lazily, mumbling about how I could sometimes be a darned nuisance when someone still wanted to sleep, but I could see that the prospect of a visit to the tile factory appealed to her. When I closed the door behind me she was already slipping her feet into her fur-trimmed slippers. I went straight to my bedroom to see what I could find to wear.

At the last moment, however, she decided not to accompany us. She was awaiting a telephone call from one of the Lisbon shops, she explained, and did not want to be out when the call finally came through. Ricardo and I protested in vain. Julieta was determined, and finally Ricardo and I left on our own.

En route to the factory, he told me many interesting things. ... That, despite the many good schools and universities, less than half of the population could read or write. ... About the wine, cork, fish and eggs which the country exported. ... And he explained in detail how the ripe olives that had recently been harvested on Dom Gil's *quinta* and many others throughout the land, would be pressed without breaking the kernels so that both the flavour and the endurance of the oil would not be compromised. It interested me to learn that one of the valuable cabinets which I so admired in my bedroom at the *palacio* on account of the extraordinary greeny-yellow sheen of the wood, was made of olive wood. I was told that the gnarled roots of the trees would be used for the manufacture of snuff boxes and other ornamental articles.

Julieta actually missed a wonderful opportunity when she decided against going with us on a tour of the factory. The manufacture of the *azulejos*, the exquisite little porcelain tiles used on a large scale throughout the land, both inside and outside many of the public and private buildings, which I had noticed in the villa and now saw again here in the Sintra factory, is an industry which the Portuguese inherited from the Moors.

The manager welcomed us with genuine kindness, and went to the trouble of making my visit as pleasant as possible; answering all my questions clearly and explaining to me every step in the manufacture of the tiles. Ricardo walked around with us, but was often left behind when he needed to talk to one or another of his workmen.

When we finally came outside again, he took me to a small wooden bench in the shade.

"We shall have to wait here a little while, Erin, because they will be offended if we do not stay for refreshments. The foreman tells me that the workmen had their spouses bake special cakes for us."

"How very kind of them, *Señhor*," I readily replied, moved by the friendly gesture. "Of course we shall wait."

He left me on my own for a moment while he went back inside again in order to consult the plant manager about something, and it was then that I again remembered Cameron's letter. I had put it in my purse to be read in Ricardo's absence.

It was the most peculiar, astonishing letter I had ever received in all my life!

"Look here, Erin," it began unceremoniously, "this affair has gone on long enough! I was prepared to give you a few months to come to your senses, but it now seems to me that by that time it might already be too late!

"Where is the girl who, when I dared to suggest that she might perhaps be going to Portugal to seek a *palacio* or a title for herself, so smugly shot back: "That will be the day! ... Heaven help me!"

This morning I received your letter at my office, and what was in it but 'Ricardo does this', and 'Ricardo does that!' ...

'Ricardo says this, and Ricardo says that!' ... Ricardo is such a wonderful guy... Ricardo has bought such a beautiful present for you. The whole missive is merely a diary of all Ricardo's wonderful sayings and absorbing comings and goings!

"And then what happened to make you suddenly decide that you no longer wanted to go to the festival with him?. How did he so suddenly become the unapproachable marquis once more?

"Expect me on the first available aircraft. Even if it is only to prove to myself that he is not making you unhappy, I'm coming at once!"

In dumb astonishment I was still sitting there inertly when Ricardo returned. Without really being aware of what I was doing, I ate some of the cakes and had a slice of tart, smiled, at the people who hovered around solicitously in the background—probably so that they could later assure those who were not able to be present, that we had enjoyed the refreshments—and I also managed to chat with Ricardo and the manager with exaggerated animation.

That Cameron could be so dictatorial! Reveal such insight! I always knew that I was an open book to him but how could he have guessed what I myself had not yet known? It was also incredible that, without any intimation, he could have known that something had happened which had made me reluctant to go to the festival!

Congratulating myself on the relaxed attitude I had succeeded in maintaining until we finally had to take leave of Ricardo's staff, I was able to thank them for the their hospitality, and as I sat staring through the car window on our way home, pretending that I did so imperturbably, I felt confident that my face revealed none of the confusion that was raging in my mind.

For this reason I was unprepared when, still about two miles away from the *palacio*, Ricardo suddenly turned off the road and brought the car to an abrupt stop among the bushes. He then very deliberately turned in his seat to face me with his face unexpectedly taut.

"And now?" His question was hardly audible. "Now what was in it that made what you were reading so upsetting?"

Because astonishment temporarily robbed me of my voice, I could only stare at him vacantly.

"What did my good friend, the *Señhor* Monroe, have to say that was bad enough to perturb you to such an extent?"

"How did you know that it was from him?" I asked childishly, prevaricating." And nothing has disturbed me. Nothing has upset me." Agonizingly aware only of the face so close to mine and the wild beating of my heart, I stammered on incoherently. "Only that he is on his way here and ... and ... Well I'm really excited. Cameron is one of my dearest friends...!"

"That I have already concluded for myself," he said dryly. "I also heard from Julieta that he was determined to marry you. So. ...." His voice suddenly hardened. "You are naturally now much concerned because you have, in addition, encouraged Carlos, raising his expectations, and because the lawyer will also soon be here, you are of course in an unenviable predicament! It looks to me as if you are going to have to come to your senses and make a decision very quickly!"

"*No, Señhor*! You have it all wrong!" I shrank from the suppressed rage in his face. "Have I not already explained that I'm not in love with Carlos? Now please believe, me once and for all, he means nothing to me!"

"Then he leaves one very little choice to believe otherwise!" The bitter, censorious note was still audible in his voice. "His own behavior creates the impression, because he plainly puts himself out to be with you as much as possible!"

"*Señhor*, do you always so summarily jump to your own conclusions? First you maintained that I had to be in love with Carlos because his interests were obviously close to my heart. Now he's suddenly in love with me! Believe me, there is no talk of anything like that. He does indeed seek out my company, but I think I know the reason for that.

"In South Africa we have a saying that 'it often it turns out to be not as much about the dog as about the collar...' and that definitely has a bearing on this matter. Carlos undoubtedly finds me a perfect ally, but, more than that he finds in me a good excuse to be close to Julieta!"

"Are you trying to tell me that Carlos cherishes romantic ideas about Julieta?" He slapped his knee with his hand and grinned delightedly, his face brightening for a moment. "Now who would ever have guessed that?" ... But now what about *Señhor* Munroe? ... Immediately his voice sounded cold again. "I wonder if you will be as clever in trying to explain that! You admit that he wants to marry you... that he is in love with you?"

"Ye...es," I began but suddenly broke off when he suddenly bent forward to take both my arms in a grip of steel.

"Do you love him, Erin?" he demanded passionately, shaking me slightly while his fingers bored into my flesh. "I must know immediately ... do you love him? I *must* know!"

"At first I did not think so, but now I'm not so sure..."

"Then I shall help you to make sure!" He muttered; his teeth clenched., and before I knew what was happening, his arms closed tightly around me and he brought his mouth down hard on mine!

"Erin ... oh, Erin!... Such uncertainty is enough to rob a man of his sanity!"

"Ricardo!" I felt as if I swam in a sea of unknown ecstasy. Passion was very new to me. He let me go and then caught me in his arms once more, kissing me again; my eyes, my hair, my lips and even my hands My heart beat madly and my entire body was weak.

"How can I let you go?" he asked at a last, but I was eager to get home. I longed for nothing more than to be alone with my thoughts so that I could relive this precious experience and analyze my feelings. I, Erin March, successful and world-wise career woman, was as naïve as a child when it came to matters of the heart!

In front of the *palacio*, I leaped out of the car and ran straight to my bedroom, where, trembling, I closed the door behind me. Still moved by the fiery caresses, I touched my lips incredulously, with cautious fingers, reliving Ricardo's passionate kisses. Frantic, and unnerved, I paced back and forth on that luxurious Chinese carpet; one thought hammering in my head: 'Ricardo had kissed me like that and yet not once had he said that he loved me!'

Bending over to look in the mirror, it surprised me to discover that I still looked the same for I felt so different. My cheeks were still flaming and the eyes looking back into mine were perhaps a little darker than usual, but if I had suddenly been obliged to go out of the door no one would have been any the wiser.

I had so often in my dreams pictured myself just like that, in Ricardo's embrace, that I should have been the happiest girl on earth—but I was not! I only felt afraid, unhappy and uncertain. Consumed with doubt.

If I could have run away at that moment, I would have done so, because inexperienced as I was, I was not sure of how I should conduct myself in future. Common sense told me that Ricardo might now see me only as a possible plaything and nothing more. ... He had taken me out alone without a chaperone; something he would never, for instance, have done with Isabella.—And then he had kissed me like that in the remoteness of the forest. In my heart I knew that he would likely conduct himself in a more orthodox manner if ever he planned to marry a girl.

I suddenly longed desperately for Cameron, or even Angela; for my own people who thought and would feel as I did. And when my thoughts went off in this direction, I again remembered Cameron's letter and was tortured by the realization that he might not be quite as indulgent in future. ... Once roused, did such quiet, gentle people ever again become quite so compliant! I recalled hastily crunching the letter and putting it back in my handbag when Ricardo had made his appearance, intending to read it once more, and I hastened to retrieve it. I followed the text of it as well as the trembling of my hands permitted and now read the last few lines, which I had missed, with rising concern!

Truly, this had been a day of shocks!

"It is probably advisable,' Cameron wrote, *'to warn you that Fernando Pereira is on his way to Portugal. Apparently he has already left by plane, having borrowed the necessary money for the ticket from the chief clerk in his office, after explaining that he was about to enter into marriage with a very rich heiress!*

"That he will contact Julieta immediately I have no reason no doubt! He must, when push comes to shove, at least make an attempt to pay back his airfare!

"Please try to make her understand how undesirable it would be or how dangerous it is for her to continue their friendship, but be very careful that you don't make her stubborn.

"Looking forward to our meeting,

"Impatient to see you,

"C. M."

With a feeling of impending disaster I went to look for Julieta. The stories attached to her unexpected desire to stay home that morning added to the mysterious telephone call that she dared not miss, had to be investigated...

Chapter Nine

Much had transpired by the time Cameron arrived in Lisbon on the following Friday. It had been a week of vital occurrences—all unforgettable.

First of all Carlos completed his first term at the university in Estoril and Ricardo invited him to come to Sintra. Next, Noël turned up for the weekend and then—as if it was the easiest thing on earth to arrange this under the noses of a house full of people—Julieta cajoled me into accompanying her to Sintra where she had arranged to meet Fernando.

I reasoned with her; begged and pleaded, but to no avail. Poor Fernando had come all the way from Moçambique to see her and the least she could do was to bid him welcome, she persistently offered as her reason for being there, and remained obdurately unmoved by all the reasons I put forward to deter her. I became quite distraught for, with all that Cam had just written still fresh in my memory, and I wanted above all to remain worthy of the trust he and Angela Meiring had invested in me.

"Why can't he look you up openly, like any other decent young man?" I asked once, at my wits end."

"Can't you understand, Erin," she exclaimed, becoming visibly annoyed. "He's afraid of doing anything that might perhaps compromise or threaten my future. Do you think he likes having to slink around here like a thief in the night? To hang around the gates in the hope that I might chance to pass by? He hates it, but what can he do? For some silly reason Auntie Angela did not like Fernando, and he says he fears that she might write to Ricardo. Until we have established whether or not that is actually the case and what she might have said to Ricardo if she has, we have to be careful. ... Do you understand now?"

Having no other choice I could only nod affirmatively and in the end it was I who arranged with Ricardo's chauffeur to take us to town.

All the way to Sintra I sat thinking about the last time I had seen Fernando Pereira at our farewell party on the balcony of my flat in Johannesburg. Undoubtedly he would not be pleased to see me with Julieta, but if he was as cunning as everybody credited him with being, he would be far too crafty to betray that.

All four of us—Cameron, the Meirings and I—had known that night that we would not be able to fool the man for ever. All that we could hope for was to discourage him for long enough to get Julieta out of the way. It was easy for him to do his own investigation, and, in addition Julieta probably wrote and told him about her cousin's open goodwill, but who would ever have dreamt that he would actually go as far as to follow her? I should have realized then that any man who was this persistent could also be dangerous in his determination.

On the day before Cameron arrived, we once again visited the café which had now become the chosen meeting place of the two. I could see that Fernando was gnashing his teeth because of my admiral talent for 'playing gooseberry', but there was little that he could do about it. Julieta too knew very well that she could not go to Sintra on her own, and, in any case, if she ever tried, Denis—her assigned driver—who regarded it as his specific duty to accompany her in the streets—would also have regarded it as his duty to report to the marquis any deviation from his orders. Temporarily I thus allowed the affair to go its own way.

There were more things to disturb my peace of mind. Whenever we were alone, Ricardo would hold his arms open to me—and I have to admit that, weak mortal that I am—I was only too willing to go to him, even if it was just to know the wild joy it gave me to hear to feel his heart beat so close to mine, and the sweet pain in my bruised lips after he had pressed his mouth so passionately on mine.

Never in the entire week was I completely happy. All the time I was aware that I was waiting for something dire to happen, but I could not foresee what that would be.

One morning while we waited for our horses to quench their thirst in the stream before we returned to the house for breakfast, he held me in an almost hopeless embrace. He brought his mouth close to my ear and I heard him groan as though he were in physical pain: "O, Erin, Erin, why did this have to happen to me? Why should I be punished like this?" And then I remembered what he had said on the night of the festival; that no matter how much a man loved a woman, he had no right to allow his heart to overrule his duty. Without speaking we sprang back into our saddles and galloped back to the house in somber silence, and when I encountered him later, standing in front of the enormous painting of his grandmother that hung in the dining room, I did not wonder any longer.

It was delightful to see Cameron again. When you have spent more than ten years of your life in the company of the same man day in and day and day out, it is natural to become accustomed to him, and now I realized even more acutely how much I had been missing him.

I met him at the airport and we were casual and impersonal when we greeted one another, but when we found ourselves in a quiet corner in the terminal and he held me at arm's length from him, we studied one another keenly and found ourselves slightly breathless. I'd forgotten that he was such an attractive man, or perhaps I had never before noticed it so forcibly.

The touch of silver at his temples which, in the past, I had regarded as a sign of the passing years, most definitely suited him. To me he looked trim and distinguished and—when I looked up into his face, tanned after many hours on the golf course—very precious. It saddened me that the possibility of a misunderstanding had to be hovering over us to threaten so great a friendship. For a moment I fervently wished that everything could once more be as it had been, and that I'd never come to Portugal, but immediately after that I knew that that was not completely true. I would never really regret that I had gone through this experience, because whatever the outcome of it all proved to be, I had at least been aroused from my old 'purposelessness.'—Henceforth I would *live* and not merely exist!

"You have lost weight, Erin," he said at last, and I knew that he was studying me just as closely as I was him. "The heat been getting you down?" He looked around inquiringly. "I see that they have not even begun to offload the luggage. Let's go and have coffee or something in the meantime."

"Ricardo has sent his personal car, Cameron," I informed him uneasily. "He could not come, himself, but he asked me to tell you that his personal driver is at your disposal for as long as you need him. And he wants you also to come and spend a few days at the *palacio*."

"Indeed? That's very nice of the man. ... The old, traditional courtesy about which I was always so eager to tell you. ... I probably wouldn't know Ricardo now."

"No probably not. *Tia* Luisa says that Carlos now reminds her very much of Ricardo as he was when he was ten years younger."

Thus the tension of our meeting was relieved, but all the while we had talked about this and that until the baggage was released by Customs, and until the *La Gonda* stopped in front of Cameron's hotel—throughout all the hours of superficial discussion—the consciousness of his last letter hovered over us like the Sword of Damocles!

While the chauffeur carried his luggage inside for him, Cameron came back to the open window next to me, and said quickly while we were still alone: "I don't think that I shall come to the *palacio* this time. The tension will probably be a bit too much for us all. But there is one favor upon which I'm going to insist. —Very soon you must spend a whole day with me in a place that will be entirely of *my* choosing. ... Will you come? ... Honestly?'

I promised...

Chapter Ten

For some reason, after returning from Lisbon after I'd gone to meet Cameron, I began almost to avoid Ricardo. I would not have been able to explain it at the time, but I think I can do so now. ... I begged Julieta to permit me to tell him about Fernando because I felt that it was perhaps due to a guilty conscience that I feared being alone with him, but she remained over-cautious. I wonder if she, herself, realized that nothing good could come of it...

"Just wait until Carlos has gone, Erin," she pleaded.

"But why?"

"We...ell, it might be easier to speak to Ricardo about it when we are alone again and the house is quiet once more. Then he won't have so many other things all going on at the same time. He has suddenly become very attached to Carlos hasn't he? They seem to be going out together quite a lot ... horse-riding, fishing, or things like that."

"That's true," I answered, adding firmly, "but I'm not going to allow you to change the subject so easily. Why do you want to see Fernando so badly? Are you perhaps in love with the man?" I could almost believe that it was Ricardo speaking! "Do you want to marry him, or what is more important—does he want to marry you?"

"Yes ... no! I don't know. You ask too many questions all the same time!"

"Well then answer them one at a time!"

She frowned thoughtfully. "I think he wants to marry me, Erin. He said so even before we left South Africa. But I'm not so sure of myself. Of course I feel very sorry for him ... or what I actually mean is... it's very romantic isn't it? The manner in which he has followed me and all that. Most other men are so slow. Take Carlos. Would he be quite so persistent?"

"I'm sure I don't know."

"I'm convinced that he would not! But be fair, Erin, how can I ever be sure if you don't ever give me a chance to be alone with Fernando? He has never even kissed me! Just give me an opportunity to make sure!"

"Portuguese girls are not expected to be sure," I remarked dryly and tried hard not to laugh. "The rule seems to be that you marry someone of whom your parents approve! Let Ricardo find you a rich count or something. Or perhaps you might still choose, Carlos!"

Always like quicksilver, she could not remain serious for very along. She shook her black curls and laughed cheerfully. "Wouldn't Carlos be furious if I didn't consult him? I like him very much, you know, Erin. He can be so much fun... but he never even looks at me, and a girl does want a bit of fire and romance, don't you agree?"

That line of discussion was beginning to be a little too risky for my liking and there I had to let it stand, but I was not surprised when, shortly after the evening meal, she slipped out though a side door of the *palacio*.

She stayed away for more than half-an-hour. By that time I was really upset. When she finally returned and tried to slip by, unseen, to go to her bedroom, I needed only one glance at those sparkling eyes before I resolutely went after her. Ricardo, Carlos, and Noël were busy playing bridge.

"Look here, Julieta, Ricardo holds me more or less responsible for you, and I don't want him perhaps to think that I encourage you to behave like this. Do that just one more time, and you need expect nothing more from me! In any case I have decided that when Carlos has returned to the University on Sunday night, I'm going to have a talk with Ricardo, and you can phone Fernando tomorrow and tell him what I have said."

If Ricardo had not been otherwise occupied I would've gone to him then and there, but as it then happened, I first raised the subject with Cameron. Julieta had upset me to such an extent that I telephoned him. I *had* to talk to somebody!

"I'm coming to fetch you early on Sunday morning, Erin," he said promptly. "And bring a hat. We're going to church!"

It was difficult to decide what to wear on the Sunday because, except for what Cam had said about going to church, I did not have the faintest idea of how he planned to pass the rest of the day. I consequently wore the same blue dress I had worn on the day I had gone to Estoril, and again wore my white hat with the wide brim..

I knew Cameron well enough to know, that if he said that he would be coming early, that was what he meant. Shortly after 7:30 am I was already dressed and walking around in the garden.

"You look cool and fresh, Erin," he remarked when he found me.

"Why does that sound to me a little like an advertisement for a cold drink?" I responded, laughing, and invited him to come inside. He greeted Ricardo warmly and both expressed their amazement at how that the years could have flown by so quickly. Then Carlos came to renew the acquaintance of a man he had last seen when he could hardly have been more than seven years old, and a few minutes later Julieta also made her appearance.

"Wonders will never cease! I'm impressed!" Carlos exclaimed teasing her. "When last were you able to see the dew on the grass, my dear little cousin?"

"I specially got up early to see *Señhor* Monro*e*," she snapped. "Show me something equally interesting another day, and I'll get up early again!"

Cam had rented a car for the day and was eager that we should be on our way; consequently we did not linger too long. Once on the highway he smiled happily and said: "This is delightful!. You will never know how long I have looked forward to this!"

Whether he referred to my company or to the fact that he was back in Portugal once more, I could not decide.

"Where are we going?" I asked a while later. "It was difficult to decide what to wear because you were not specific about the other kind of places to which we were going, and I didn't know whether we were going to church this morning or this evening!"

"We are on our way there now," he responded, "and your outfit is most suitable for any occasion. But then of course you never look anything but charming to me!" After that I felt better and eagerly began to look forward to the day ahead of us. Along the way he explained that we were going to spend the day in a little town on the border of Coimbra, his favorite place in all of Portugal.

"If you only knew how often I have wished that I could show it to you, my dear Erin! By the way I did ask Carlos if we could not save him tonight's train journey back to Coimbra, but he reminded me that tomorrow is a public holiday and that he does not have to return to the university until tomorrow night .

Some details of that day, like pieces of a well-loved Jigsaw Puzzle, will linger in my heart and my memory for as long as I live. ... The Service, conducted in a language, foreign but no longer quite so unfamiliar to me, in that dark convent church so rich in history... the flickering flames of the many candles in their golden candlesticks... the black cloaks covering the heads and shoulders of the peasant women ... the heavy smell of incense...! Those are all impressions of a day that can instantly be recalled whenever I hear the name, *Santa Clara*.

The early-morning mist was already beginning to dissipate in the sun when we came outside again. Gradually it disappeared from the crowding rooftops of Coimbra and for a little while hung over the Mondego River before it disappeared altogether, leaving the water to sparkle like a silver ribbon in the April sunshine.

Cameron had provided for everything. There was a rug, and pillows, a basket full of the most delicious food which he had persuaded the manager of his hotel to provide for us, and even a bottle of chilled Portuguese champagne. We spread the blanket out under the trees and everyone who passed back and forth along the river paths, greeted us with a friendly word, a smile or an old-fashioned bow. Now and then a small boat drifted by. Near us, on the opposite bank, two lads still in their 'Sunday Best', sat fishing.

When he could no longer resist the temptation, Cam rolled up his trouser legs and, like a naughty boy waded in the water, and it was not too long before I also went and removed my shoes and stockings in the car to do the same. Once my foot slipped and there was a moment, when he caught me in his arms so that I could regain my balance, that I had the strangest feeling that the world stood still. Involuntarily I held my breath and wondered if he was perhaps about to kiss me. Then a cry from the opposite bank called his attention to break the tension. One of the boys had caught a gigantic fish!

In his halting Portuguese, Cameron called out across the water to them, and not long after that the lads arrived, panting, with two lines which they had fetched from their homes, and also a can of the most revolting worms for us to use as bait.

"*Boa fortuna*[8] *...Señhor ... Señorita!*" They laughed, teeth white in their dark young faces.

But the creatures just refused to bite—and I maintained that it was Cameron's singing that frightened them off. Whatever the reason, we grew tired of that and went to console ourselves with cold chicken and champagne. It was a day of sunshine and blissful happiness. We let down our hair under the trees, sang and laughed a great deal.

"It's glorious here," I sighed contentedly, late in the afternoon when I had rinsed the last of the dishes in the river. ... "What made you think of a picnic, Cam?" I threw myself down on the blanket next to him and turned on my stomach in order to see him better.

"I spent many days here when I was last in Portugal and I'm only grateful that, with the passage of time, it has changed so little. You must already have guessed that I'm somewhat sentimental about this place. May I tell you the story of Santa Clara?"

"Most certainly. I'm very keen to hear it."

I of course expected that he was going to tell me the tragedy of his life; of a beautiful girl—perhaps a Portuguese peas-

---

8   Good luck

ant. Instead, I was very soon engrossed in the most tragic tale I'd ever heard in my life.

Cameron lay on his back and we stayed there, watching the sky become rosy in the West. Unnoticed, he had surreptitiously kept wriggling closer and closer until his head rested on my lap.

"Whether it is completely true, or possibly only partly so," he began, "I've never been able to ascertain, but one thing is certain. There really was once a king of Portugal, known as 'Pedro the Just'—but also as 'Pedro the Cruel.'

"Sometimes history seems very cold because the experts who set it down for future generations to read, inevitably omit to record the clashing emotions, the tragedies, and the passions that make people who and what they really are."

He had always been able to tell a story well. In my imagination the main characters and the entire tragedy came to life. I could see it all.

"Portugal was a small country in the 14th century; heavily populated and merciless. The Moors were in Granada and the shadow of Castile, the arch enemy, hung over the Portuguese. She had come from Castile, the cousin of the princess who was married to Pedro, the young Crown Prince of Portugal, and their love was inevitable as the death which nearly brought the story to an end. ... Nearly— but not quite!

"Long after she had been murdered, when Pedro had become king," Cameron continued, "he remained as one possessed. He was determined that his Inez, his beloved, his darling, would yet be accepted as their queen by the people who had murdered her, no matter what!

"He had her exhumed and in the church of Santa Clara the bones were crowned with the royal crown of Portugal. The cream of Portuguese nobility were made to kneel before that pathetic little skeleton and kiss what had once been the lovely, gracious little hand of Inez!"

"How ghastly!" I whispered, shuddering. "And how utterly demented his grief must have made him to drive him to go to such lengths!"

"Precisely! That's just what I meant. I wonder how many history books portray the craziness that lay behind his misdeeds! There is a story, a legend perhaps, about how one person knelt down to kiss her foot and a toe broke off in his hand"

"And that is where we were this morning," I murmured pensively. "Is it still the same church ... the same building?"

"I really don't know."

Involuntarily I turned my head in that direction to look towards it. "I must remember to ask Ricardo when we get home tonight."

Sad how one ill-chosen word can spoil everything. The moment I had said it I was already regretting it—but by then it was already too late. ... Ominously an unfamiliar, closed expression crept across Cameron's face. He rose to his feet angrily and very deliberately began to dust the grass off his sleeves.

"Yes. That's right! Go and ask him by all means! He will most definitely know. Doesn't he know *everything*?"

"No, Cam," I tried clumsily to placate him "Please don't take that the wrong way. I only meant ... well, it is, after all, his country and he would be expected to know such things, but if you would rather I did not ask him, I shall of course forget it!"

He bent over and capriciously began to pack up our belongings. "My dear Erin, you are perfectly entitled to do as you choose. Come, let us now talk about something else!"

But I was already close to tears because our lovely day had been spoiled and was ending in this way. Disappointment made me peevish and, woman-like, I would not rest until he had been punished for that!

"Now you're being childish, Cameron. I was unaware that you could be so touchy. ... I don't know what's come over you lately!"

"That's right! Pile all the blame onto me," he said sarcastically as he walked towards the car. "But then of course we can't all be perfect. Unfortunately we're not all Ricardo's!"

"Please leave Ricardo out of this! I don't know what he has to do with the subject."

"I don't either. I had begun to wonder how long it would be before you would somehow drag his name into the conversation. It's become second nature with you. ... Every sentence usually begins with, 'Ricardo does this and Ricardo does that.' I don't know why I waste my time on you!"

Men are so obstinate! He had begun the whole thing, but would he ever admit it? A red haze of fury appeared before my eyes. When I get to be really angry, I'm not responsible for what I say.

"And what about it?" I demanded passionately. "There is a saying in Scripture that tells us that the mouth overflows out of the abundance of the heart!"

Cameron looked up, furious. He set the basket down and took a threatening step forward.

"You little..." he began through clenched teeth and grabbed hold of me. He pressed my head back and kissed me until I stopped squirming and relaxed in his arms. "It is I whom you love, and you know it!" And then he let me go so unexpectedly that I staggered backwards. Perversely he stood laughing at me.

"Oh!" I panted, furious and helpless. "You are impossible!"

He only laughed the louder.

"Listen to me, Cameron Monroe," I cried hoarsely, and stamped my foot emphatically while I swallowed to rid myself of the lump in my throat. "I would not look at you even if you were the last man on earth!"

At that his expression immediately changed and he regarded me coldly. "Say that again, Erin," he warned me, speaking very slowly. "Pride is not completely foreign to me, although you obviously think so. Say that one more time and it will be the last. I assure you that I shall never again bore you with my presence."

"I hate you," I yelled, now completely beside myself. "I would not look at you if you were the last man on earth!"

His hand closed around my wrist in a grip of iron and then he dragged me determinedly towards the car. "Get in," he commanded coldly and slammed the door shut before he went back to pick up the basket. "I'm taking you home before your Don Juan sets the police on my track!"

We traveled the whole distance in silence while I sat fighting back tears before I remembered what the original purpose of our meeting had been.

"We haven't yet talked about Julieta," I ventured meekly as we were driving through the gates of the *palacio*. "She's now beginning to meet Fernando on the quiet and I really don't know what to do about it."

"Ask Ricardo," he snapped back. "He will know!'

"But I'm too scared to tell him about it. What can I say to him?"

"My dear Erin, is this not the most priceless romance? I would not dream of taking on this case in court for a million pounds sterling. You don't like deceiving, him but he has once more become so awe-inspiring that you are afraid to talk to him!—Sorry! I'm getting tired of the whole business and I'm leaving the lot of you to sort out the problem for yourselves!"

For a moment I still hoped that it was not too late to make things right between us, but he had already turned on the ignition, and grinding the gears in his haste to get away, he could not hear my voice above the noise. It was only when, sobbing, I turned around to go inside, that I noticed Ricardo waiting for me on the top step...

One look at Ricardo's face in the gathering dusk and I thought at once that something very dire must have happened. I wondered anxiously if he had perhaps found out about Julieta and Fernando and held me responsible.

Wordlessly he took me by the by the hand and led me to his study, the one room in the whole house that no one ever entered without an invitation. He closed the door very carefully behind him, put my hat, gloves and handbag carefully down on his desk, and then he turned around to wrap his arms convulsively around me.

"Erin!" His voice was hoarse. "Erin!" He cried again, and kissed me as if he would never let me go again.

"Ricardo!" I tried to protest, but every word was smothered by his lips. I was startled by the expression on his face. "Ricardo, I can hardly breathe!" Suddenly penitent, he allowed me to escape from his embrace. He dragged an armchair closer for me and went to sit on a low seat at my feet. When I looked up in his eyes, I was moved by the unusual humility I suddenly read in them.

"Erin, *querida*," he said gently, with a crooked smile that made tears sting my eyes, "allow me to confess that those members of my family whom I condemned so readily, were no weaker than I, myself. Today I nearly went out of my mind here with the thought of you and Cameron. ... I can no longer go on like this!" He took my hand and pressed his mouth tenderly to my palm. "What I am asking, my darling, is that you marry me!"

For the second time in less than two weeks shock robbed me of my voice. Almost panic-stricken, I looked around me and desperately wondered what to say. It is impossible to describe the confusion that suddenly raged in my mind. For a long time I had tortured myself because he did not say these very words, and now that they had been said all I wanted to do was flee!

Without waiting for an answer he rose and frenetically began to pace back and forth.

"It is so easy to judge other people," he said, almost as if it were to himself that he was talking, "and who is the fool who derides temptation as long as it is the other man who is being led into it? With you constantly in the vicinity I have behaved myself as recklessly as Carlos or any lovesick peasant boy. ... I can neither sleep nor eat well! I can hardly converse naturally with Noël, because I'm constantly only aware of you ... the fair loveliness that I *must* possess!" He shrugged his shoulders with a gesture of helplessness. "You most probably retain very little admiration for me."

I could sincerely sympathize with him because had I not also realized too late what power there lies in mutual attraction—although it might only be physical? And especially when all the time that feeling is being nurtured, pampered and cherished? I understood very well, but it is awful to see a proud man robbed of his pride. What particularly disturbed me was that he should be so unhappy: I could almost say that he was in tremendous agony of spirit. For a moment he almost helped me forget my own dilemma.

But there was yet another situation that I was compelled to take seriously because all of sudden I knew what had been bothering me for so long. Even if I had not been blessed with this unforgettable day with Cameron—marriage to Ricardo was unthinkable!

We had nothing in common, not even our language; and how would I ever fit properly into the rôle of 'Marquise da Monsaraz' when I was already longing so desperately for my friends, for my own people; for Cameron and Angela, and for the thorn trees of the Transvaal. Would the mountains around Sintra, magnificent as they were, satisfy me? In the dark corners of my mind there would always be a vestige of doubt; furthermore I now knew that it was Cameron who had subconsciously withheld me from taking an irrevocable step even though Ricardo's kisses had been so stirring.

"Please don't make yourself unnecessarily unhappy, Ricardo," I pleaded at last. "You are not the only one who was captivated. We're only human..."

"You also felt it, Erin!" he interjected eagerly; one minute remaining as though rooted to the floor, only to rush forward the next, to kneel before me on the floor. "You felt it too!... How was I expected to withstand it? But you still don't understand completely. ... You have no perception of my pitiful weakness. I have played the judge over Carlos and Julieta, asked you to be my wife, while I ... how can I say this, my *pequena*? I am already engaged Isabella!" In dumb bewilderment I had to listen as he explained how, before Julieta and I had come to Lisbon, he and Isabella had decided to keep their engagement quiet until her term of mourning was over.

"I beg of you not to look at me like that, Erin" he pleaded. "I assure you there was never any talk of love. None of the fiery passion that we have known, *Querida*. You have no idea how unpleasant life can be for a young woman who becomes a widow. Miguel da Silva was my greatest friend; Isabella my beloved little cousin. I never expected ever to find a girl with whom I could fall in love..."

But he had misinterpreted the expression on my face and my obvious consternation. I would never be able to describe to anybody a situation of mingled grief and relief such as I now experienced!

I had once, long ago, felt more or less like that, in the days when I still derived so much joy and pleasure from the collection of lovely things in my apartment. I had gone to an art exhibition the previous week, where I fell in love with a painting by the eminent South African artist, Theunis de Jongh, which I definitely could not afford. It had been put aside provisionally for other people, and for more than a week I was quite sick with worry that they might get it and not I. Eventually, needing to put an end to my misery, I scraped together the courage and went into the gallery to inquire about the painting. When I learned that it had been sold on the previous day, I was not even disappointed. In contrast with what one would have expected, my only reaction was one of intense relief because I no longer had to concern myself about something which, when I came to think of it, was completely out of my reach.

With the necessary way out now open to me, I had just begun to tell Ricardo that I thought far too much of *Dom* Gil to do anything like that to his daughter, when the phone on Ricardo's desk rang. Before I could make it clear that it I considered that it would have been cruel to treat Isabella like that— that we could not possibly be the cause of yet another upheaval in her young life—he went to lift the receiver, and informed me a moment later that the call was for me.

Reacting to the wildest hope that it might be Cameron, that it was still not too late for the situation between us to be resolved, I sprang up eagerly from my chair, but that Sunday had not yet delivered all the shocks that were in store for me. "I'll take the call in my bedroom, Ricardo," I said hastily when I recognized the voice and went quickly through the door. It was Fernando Pereira!

"But I can't possibly come now!" I protested indignantly when he made this ridiculous demand known to me. "The gong for the evening meal will sound within half-an-hour or so, and *Dom* Ricardo will wonder why I'm not at the table. ... He will feel downright insulted. Besides, I've been out for the whole day and I'm dead tired."

"My heart bleeds for you of course, Miss March," the obnoxious voice crackled mockingly in my ear, "Nevertheless, all apologies leave me cold. I must make it clear to you that I expect you before 7:45. The taxi is already on its way and will wait for you at the big gate!"

"I shall not come!" I answered firmly.

"Do as you please!" There was something ominous in the tone of voice which he now adopted. "If that is your firm decision, I promise you that I shall personally see to it that you—and Julieta—regret it for the rest of your lives!

"I am talking to you from a telephone booth in the middle of nowhere, and the taxi driver is out of earshot so don't bank on anyone finding out where I am!"

What could I do? There was no other choice open to me! Taking a quick look at the time I snatched up a light jacket, found a scarf to tie around my head, said a hasty prayer that I would be back in time for dinner, and very quietly went out through the same side door that Julieta had used two nights before.

In the dark, I stumbled over every possible loose stone but dared not be deterred. When I came around a corner in the long, winding path which lead from the house to the main road, I saw the lights of the taxi waiting for me in the distance. At that moment, as never before, I wished that I had never, ever decided to leave South Africa!

Not everything Fernando said to me, and certainly not my impolite remarks, are important; the crux of the matter was simply that Julieta had, as requested, informed him of what I'd said regarding my decision to tell Ricardo about everything that night, and he was determined that I would be prevented from doing so. Of far greater interest, in my opinion, was the fact that Ricardo had meanwhile become impatient and decided to go and look for me in my bedroom. Wasn't it reckless of me to have left the *palacio* without leaving behind any sort of apology?

As I heard later, he was naturally concerned when he discovered that I was nowhere to be found in the house. It was while he was outside in the garden calling out to me, that Denis, the driver who had been assigned to Julieta, came upon him. I can clearly picture what happened after that!

That Denis had also seen the lights near the gate, was only just one more in a series of coincidences. He had gone to investigate, he reported, and had seen a woman running in that direction.

"I'm sure that it was the *Señorita* Erin, *Señhor* Marquis," he maintained. "Perhaps she has quickly gone to Sintra again, in the taxi. The vehicle was definitely going in the direction."

"What could she be going to do there at the time of the night? She knows no one there..."

April in Portugal

"But I have taken her and the *Señorita* Julieta there frequently in the Mercedes this week. She always goes to the same place."

After that he must have volunteered to take Ricardo to the café where we had been accustomed to meeting Pereira. I think I also know why Ricardo had not first gone to speak to Julieta about this. It could have been that he expected to find her with me but more probably did not want anyone else to know about it because if it all turned out to be a fiasco, he would look exceedingly ridiculous!

Meanwhile, there was I; unsuspecting and unaware of how quickly matters were beginning to reach a climax, trying in vain to reason with Fernando Pereira. Too late did I begin to appreciate the hopelessness, as well as the danger of my situation. Pereira was completely unprincipled. That I would agree and promote his marriage to Julieta, was unthinkable—but what was the alternative?

"No one would ever connect me with you if you were to disappear without a trace," he mocked me, confident in the knowledge that he driven me into a corner.

"The man with the taxi?" I suggested, trying to a confidence that I certainly was far from feeling.

"Money can seal even the most eager mouth, my dear Miss March. I assure you that that part of the matter was settled long ago!"

"Cameron Munro, will connect you with my disappearance" I suddenly remembered, with rising hope. ... He knows all about you. I spent the day with him and he also knows that I was planning to tell the marquis about you tonight."

He smiled dangerously, not deterred in the least. "Pretending that it is out of the question to abduct you—remember I said 'pretend,' because I still don't admit that I'm convinced—there's still a way out for me. You keep quiet, and I'll keep quiet, but just open your mouth and it will at once become my duty to tell the marquis as well as his dear little niece about *your* deceit. It will provide me a great deal of pleasure to tell them that you traded on Julieta's attachment to you and used your influence over her as a means to an end!"

"But that's not true!"

"Isn't it? I'm not too sure of that. But, in any case, what difference does it make now, whether it's true or not? My imagination can easily fill in the missing details of the intrigue."

"They will never believe you." I was sure of that. "Both the marquis and Julieta would simply laugh at you if you dared to hint at anything like that."

"I wonder!" Obviously nothing I could say would have the necessary effect of shocking him out of that terrifying self-confidence. "A girl of her age, particularly one with Julieta's temperament, can fly off the handle very quickly at the slightest hint that someone else might perhaps be perching on her preserves...!"

"You shameless cad!" I cried. "As if any woman with a smattering of common sense would look at you!"

"Hush, Miss March! Fancy interrupting so impolitely! ... As I was about to say, it wouldn't be difficult to get Julieta into such a state that you would find it almost impossible to get her to listen to reason. The Marquis does not present any problem to me either. What man who is as proud as he is would like to think that a woman had been leading him by the nose for what she can get out of him?"

"Every minute detail of that café—from the red and white checkered tablecloths on the tables to the candle grease that ran down the fat green bottles that served as candlesticks—will probably remain in my memory forever. Scores of people around me. In the smoky background the orchestra dressed in

Gypsy costumes, and beside our table a mirror so large that it enabled me to see the table on the sidewalk outside without having to turn my head.

Scores around me indeed, but not one familiar face among them; each patron too engrossed in the menu or the piled plates of food in front him or her, to pay any attention to me. Could I possibly go to one of those strangers and say in my limited Portuguese: "Help me please. My companion is a scoundrel who is bent on doing me harm!" Of course I could not! I could not believe that it was I, Erin March, who sat there. The situation was like a nightmare or a ridiculous scene from a far-fetched American thriller!

Desperate, I was sitting there staring fixedly in front of me when suddenly, out of the corner of my eye I saw hope reflected in the mirror in the form of a distinctive and very welcome cream-colored *La Gonda*. I waited only long enough to make sure that it was indeed Ricardo's before calling out urgently to him. How he had got there I didn't know and I didn't care. I was only so relieved to see him. With a cry of joy I jumped up and ran outside.

There could have been wings on my feet as I fled towards him, but a further shock awaited me. For a moment he looked incredulously into my eyes, and then, thoroughly disillusioned—judging by his expression—from me to the man behind me, before he turned around without a word, and strode back to his car.

For more than a minute I clean forgot about Fernando Pereira. I was aware only of that red light disappearing in the distance. Then I heard the voice behind me.

"Now we shall see whom they believe," he sneered.

Just then a taxi dropped off passengers next to me and, seizing the opportunity, I almost fell into it.

"To the Palacio da Monsaraz!" I was saying when Fernando caught up with me, and he had the nerve to squeeze in beside me.

"You're not going without me!" he muttered under his breath, pulling the door closed after him.

In such a mood, and in the powerful La Gonda, Ricardo was home long before us, and he went straight to Julieta's bedroom to ascertain whether she could shed some light on the whole crazy situation. Unfortunately, like a startled rabbit she was too afraid to open her mouth and promptly decided that the safest thing to do would be to behave as if she were completely ignorant. She thus maintained that she knew nothing...

"Why don't you ask Erin?"

It was then that he told her that I had been in Sintra with a strange man; one whom, according to Denis, she too, had visited with me, and somehow she succeeded in hiding her dismay. "Why don't you wait until she comes home and ask yourself?" she suggested.

But that was precisely what he was *not* planning to do. I believe that as he felt then, he would rather have died than ever have to see me again. His pride was ever his Achilles' Heel, and one thing he would never forgive, was that anyone should make a fool of him. The shock of my perceived deceit was bad enough, but that I had dragged Julieta along with me, under false pretenses, was the last straw. Without informing anyone except Noël of his intentions, he stormed into his room, threw a few things into a suitcase and took off in the La Gonda for Estoril.

I know exactly how he must have felt. Often when we are distressed about something, we only want to be left alone to think; and how distraught he must have been! Less than an hour before that he had, in that very house, asked me to be his wife—the greatest honor it was in his power to bestow on anyone. And I had not even waited long enough to respond to his proposal before I was secretly on my way to go and meet another man—or that is how it must have appeared to him. Circumstances decidedly made my behavior appear immeasurably worse...

Of his decision to go to the villa in Estoril, I knew nothing, however, and it was with a certain amount of surprise that I saw Julieta standing alone on the top step. With a characteristic lack of shame Fernando brazenly followed me into the house.

"Erin!" Julieta cried anxiously; both uncertainty and reproach detectable in her voice. "Wherever have you been all this time?" That was when she caught sight of Fernando. In the light on the veranda her face was unusually pale; only one flaming red blotch burned on each cheek. ... Julieta was jealous!

Suddenly I was too tired to talk. It had been a long, exhausting day, with one evil after another, and I doubted that my nerves could stand another. Was it really only that morning that I had left there looking forward with such blissful expectation to the day with Cameron? It could've been years ago! My knees were weak when we reached the top step.

I still expected to find Ricardo inside. The frightening Ricardo who, without a word, had left me standing on the sidewalk in front of the café... the strange Ricardo with a dark, cold eyes and thin lips. It had been cowardly of me not to have stood my ground, I admit readily, but I really could not take any more.

"Answer me, Erin!" Julieta commanded, now really angry.

With a tired hand I swept the damp hair from my forehead. "I'm tired of the whole sorry business now," I managed to say, precisely as Cameron had said shortly before that. "Rather go and ask Fernando to explain. I'm going to my room!" And with a sob I ran into the house!

It was only when it was too late, that I realized how unwise it had been of me to provide Fernando with such a golden opportunity, but I was so worn out by then and of course there was still the very faint hope that Ricardo or Julieta—or perhaps both—would refuse to listen to his stories. Besides, I could think of nothing that Fernando could possibly say to make things worse than they were already. Because I did not have his monstrous powers of imagination, I could not even begin to dream of how he would swing the situation to his advantage.

He told Julieta that I had relentlessly pursued him; that I had always run after him, and out of sheer envy would try to drive a wedge in between them. Apparently while we were still in Johannesburg I had made him a promise that if he would only wait for me, everything that I could get out of the wealthy Marquis, would be his.

Gullible little Julieta, confused and tragically disillusioned, unfortunately accepted that all I had ever said against Fernando, only supported his accusation.

I was sitting in darkness at my window when she burst in, uninvited, and turned on the light. Before she was able speak, she had to take a few deep breaths. I think that rage had overwhelmed her. Then she let fly and both Portuguese and English alternately streamed in a flood from her lips.

"Julieta!" I suddenly felt so very sad. "Please don't leave here in that frame of mind. Your friendship is very precious to me, and I think that the least you can do is to give me an opportunity to defend myself before you jump to any conclusions. You will never know how unhappy you have made me tonight!" I could have reminded her of how much, including my career and my apartment, I had given up for her. ... That I had traveled thousands of miles from my homeland for her sake, but pride restrained me.

"You can go to the devil for all I care!" she shouted wildly. "I don't care a damn about whether you are happy or not. Did you ever take my happiness into consideration while you were trying to steal Fernando from me? Don't think for a moment that I did not see you on the balcony on the night of your farewell party...!"

"Julieta!" I tried vainly to pacify her, but by degrees my own temper was beginning to rise. I was, after all, not a child, and who was she to be screaming at me? "If I were you I'd be a little more careful of what you say!"

I'd heard and read much about the fiery Latin temperament but that night was a revelation to me. Angry as she was, I was nevertheless unprepared for the effect my last remark had upon her.

"Take your things and get yourself away from here immediately!" She had lost complete control of herself and stepped forward threateningly. "You're not worthy of my friendship or Ricardo's! Either you go or I will.—This house, as enormous as it is, is simply not big enough for both of us!"

This was just too much for me. The last straw! After all I also have pride, although I do not like to talk about it as much as they do. My chair scraped across the floor as I pushed it back, and I raised my chin defiantly.

"Please leave, Julieta," I requested, deathly calm, and gritted my teeth. "You're unfortunately in my way and I want to pack!'

Although it would not have made any difference to my determination to leave, I was still hoping against hope that at the last minute Ricardo would come to apologize. Even towards his servants he was always politeness and courtesy itself and I just could not believe that he would let me go without a farewell greeting, no matter how cold. Had he not said that he loved me?

If it had been possible I would have liked to thank him for his hospitality, but, unable to do so, I had to be content—before closing the door of the room with all that beautiful furniture, forever—with writing him a little note, expressing feelings that I would not have the privilege to say to him personally.

I walked down the passage carrying my smaller cases to see if I could not perhaps find Inez or her husband, José, hoping that they could call a taxi for me and make arrangements for the rest of my luggage to be carried out, when unexpectedly I bumped into Carlos. I'd forgotten all about him.

"What are you still doing here?" I asked him before I could recall what Cam had told me about the following day being a holiday.

"You rather tell me what you are doing here in the passage at 9:30 in the evening with a suitcase in each hand?" He smiled, one eyebrow questioningly arched.

"Is it already so late?" I asked evasively. I'd begun to wonder if the day would ever come to an end.

"It is... but that doesn't answer my question!"

To my distress my mouth suddenly began to quiver, my eyes blurred, and no matter how I battled to avoid this, two big tears ran down my cheeks. I smiled hesitantly. "There has been a spot of trouble, Carlos, and I'm going away!"

"What?... Run that by me again." He took the suitcases out of my hands and set them down on the floor. "Trouble? What sort of trouble and with whom?"

"Go and ask Julieta," is all that I was able to say. Embarrassed, I was frantically digging around in my handbag.

"Here!" He gave me his handkerchief. "Take this one in the meantime and wait here. I'll be back in a moment!"

How shall I ever forget Carlos's kindness that night? He was like a wild animal when he returned a few minutes later.

"They're crazy!" he remarked briefly. "Stark staring mad! ... I don't blame you for one moment if you want to get away from here!" He picked up the suitcases that were still where he had set them down shortly before that, and began to walk on ahead of me. "And who is the greasy-faced individual with Julieta?"

"Fernando Pereira. He is the cause of all the unpleasantness. Please don't ask me to ask to explain to you now, Carlos," I begged, running to keep up with him. "I promise to explain everything when I'm not quite as weary as I am now."

"One look at him was enough to unsettle me, too!" Suddenly he stood still and looked compassionately into my eyes "We shall most definitely talk about this again, Erin. They can't be allowed to treat you like this. One thing is certain, whatever you decide now, you're not going alone. You have been too good to me to deserve that. I would have been leaving here tomorrow night in any case."

Outside he left me alone for a short while.

"Where are you going?" I called out after him.

"To look for Denis. If we are leaving here, we're at least going to leave in style. We are not going in any taxi."

He went with me to the hotel in Lisbon where Julieta and I had stayed before we departed for Sintra, and he waited until the night clerk had ascertained that a room was available for me. Then he went up the stairs with me and accompanied me right into my bedroom.

"Well," he said cheerfully, doubtless in the hope that by so doing he could dispel my despair, "it looks clean and comfortable. Is there anything thing else I can do for you before I go to the station?"

There was nothing. He had already done more for me than he would ever know. Exhausted as I was I could certainly not have managed by myself.

"I am more than grateful ..." I began, and then came the reaction. I subsided into the nearest chair, covering my face with my hands, and cried as if my heart would break. Concerned, Carlos came and stood next to me and in his unpractised way tried to comfort me.

"Never mind! Never mind!" he said repeatedly, and clumsily stroked my hair. "It will all come right—just wait and see! Don't be so unhappy!"

The next moment I must have sounded like a child who saw that the world was in flames, and yet cried because her doll was not wearing a clean dress!

"I'm crying about *Cameron*," I wailed forlornly. "I'm crying because I quarreled with him!"

At that Carlos unexpectedly snatched up his hat. "I'll have to hurry, Erin. It's getting late. I hope that Denis is still waiting outside."

"Where are you going?" I asked unnecessarily. "To the station?"

"To find Cameron Monroe, of course. Why did you not speak sooner?"

"But you don't know where to find him!"

"Oh, yes, I do!" he replied from outside in the passage, He has invited me to have dinner with him on Wednesday night. I have his address!"

Chapter Eleven

The week that followed was certainly the longest and most wretched of my entire life. I did not know a soul in that big, foreign city. Loneliness very soon became a dull, gnawing pain, that was as much physical as emotional. Strangely enough and probably from force of habit, in the midst of my misery I was concerned about Julieta—and I could only hope that she would not go and do anything foolish.

In addition, I was concerned about my financial situation. I still had enough money for my trip back home, but if I stayed in the hotel much longer I would be obliged to use some of that. Only the longing to see Cameron one more time before I left, and my firm belief that he would not disappoint me, kept me in Lisbon.

But Cam did not come!

I went down to the public telephone in the foyer more than once and lifted the receiver, only to set it down again despondently without dialing. Carlos had surely told him about the situation in which I found myself, I kept telling myself, and if he wanted to come, he would!

By the Thursday of that week, I was seriously considering trying to find employment somewhere. There were several

English-speaking firms in the city, and some of the schools would possibly have an opening for a shorthand and typing teacher.

On the Friday I took a taxi to the library and spent nearly the whole day there searching through newspapers without finding a single position for which I could apply.

On Saturday afternoon I wandered listlessly through the park opposite the hotel, and finally went to sit down on one of the benches. I had, however, before departing from the hotel, taken the precaution of leaving a message at the front desk, so that Cameron would know where to find me if perhaps he came to look for me during my absence. I still refused, albeit no longer quite as emphatically, to give up hope. He was deeply hurt, I told myself repeatedly, and consoled myself with the thought that when his anger had subsided, he would surely come.

But in the park, alone among so many strangers, my courage suddenly deserted me. It seemed to me that I was the only person in the whole place that did not even have a dog for company. I sat there wondering if it would not be more advisable for me to book a berth on a ship and go back home—and it was that word 'home' that was finally my undoing.

How I mourned that flat and all the lovely things that were no longer mine! Would I ever again have my own little place? What prospects now awaited me in Johannesburg? Where would I live, and would Cameron take me back?— No. ... It could not be expected of Suzanne Tredoux to stand aside in favor of me...

Self-pity suddenly overcame me to such an extent that in front of all those people I unashamedly permitted tears to roll freely, down my cheeks. "Admit it, Erin," I admitted to myself, "you have lost him for ever!"

Why did Carlos also not even bother to send me a message? Everyone, *everyone* had forsaken me!

And that is how Carlos found me just after five that afternoon.

"Good gracious, Erin," he remarked good-naturedly. "You're surely not still crying, after all this time?"

"You silly thing!" I smiled through my tears. "Where have you come from?"

"From Sintra. I arrived there last night, but this is the first opportunity I have found to come and see you. They told me at the hotel that I would find you here."

Just the very fact that I was no longer quite so alone, made me feel better. I dried my eyes and moved up so that he could sit next to me on the bench. All around us mothers were calling out to their children to come home. In the cypress tree nearby a dove had begun to coo.

Carlos took a letter from his pocket. "This arrived at the *palacio*—for you," he said. "Read it while I go and buy cigarettes. I'll be back in a minute!"

It was from Angela Meiring. I wonder if she ever could have guessed, while she sat in her lovely home in Johannesburg writing the letter to me, at what a psychological moment it would reach me. How skillfully, with her wonderful insight, she was able to put into words that perversity in my nature that had always been my downfall!

"Dearest Erin," she wrote, "By this time you're probably really displeased with me because I've not been writing, but only today could I decide what to say to you."

Dear Angela! She wrote as she spoke; with long, involved sentences. I could almost see the attractive, laughing face beside me.

"*Cameron was here a while ago and is really undone because he suspects that the fascinating Marquis is rapidly winning his girl away from him. But I quickly reassured him. I said to him: "Cam, the sooner Erin gets a few love affairs behind her, the better for you. She first needs to become aware of the fact that men exist, before she can decide on one in particular. First give her a chance to find out how great a difference there is between infatuation and love, so that she can tell the difference between them!*

"What I really meant, my friend, is that only experience teaches one to discern whether you really love a man or you are just 'in love!' A woman might fall in love dozens of times before she really learns to love one man in particular, and what I specially wanted to make him understand is that unless he happens to be the man in a million for you, it will not help him to try and fight fate.

"Please don't take offense because I speak so directly—you know how I carry your welfare in my heart—but, personally, I think that it would be good for you if the attractive Ricardo swept you off your feet.—Something like that should have happened to you years ago. How I wish I could be there to see it happen! You always intimidate men, but if and when you finally come across one that succeeds in getting under your skin, it will go to your head like champagne! Why? Because he would present a challenge! Please be careful, dearest friend, that you don't perhaps fall in love with any man just because he is difficult to capture! I remember only too well how it always was with me. As long as I had to run after o someone, it was still okay, but the moment he wanted to kiss me, there was no longer any fun in the chase! I'm sure I must have been a hunter in my previous life!"

With a half-smile on my face, I put the letter in my pocket, intending to read the bits of news and Johannesburg gossip later. I already had enough to think about.

In the distance I saw Carlos approaching, and noticed that there was something strange in his demeanor. When he came closer, I observed what I had not seen earlier because I was so absorbed in my own problems, that he was unusually pale with dark shadows under his eyes

"What's wrong, Carlos?" I asked as soon as he sat down beside me. "You look as if you haven't slept for ages!"

"Well I certainly didn't sleep last night—and that's a fact!" He lit a cigarette, which I had never known him to do before, and smoked in silence. for a moment. Then he unexpectedly turned around to look at me and said with apparent carelessness: "Julieta is going to marry that Fernando guy, Erin. Did you know?"

"Of course I didn't. Who would have told me? I am sure of one thing, however, and that is that she is not in love with him!"

The eager anticipation with which he leaned forward brought tears to my eyes.

"What makes you say so, Erin? How do you know? Has Julieta ever said anything to you that might cause you to suspect that?"

Poor Carlos! I placed my hand gently on his. "I saw long ago how things were with you. I can well understand how you feel, and it would also upset me if that marriage were actually to take place—but why were you so slow, man?"

He shrugged his shoulders. "You know how it is. ... She is on the verge of inheriting an enormous amount of money, while I. ... Who knows what will become of me!"

"That wretched money!" I cried angrily. "One man wants her for her anticipated fortune while, for that same reason, she is supposedly beyond your reach! Good heavens!" I waved aside the cigarette which, unaware of the two shocked old ladies who sat opposite us, he absentmindedly offered me. I'll tell you where pride has got the pair of you."

"Yes, but what if she really loves the other fellow. You were about to tell me why you think that that is not the case!'"

"I'm positive that she does not love Fernando.—She's flattered by his attention and she, silly, innocent little thing that she is, thinks that she knows everything about life. If you ask me, she is probably in quite a panic now because things have reached this stage. ... Fernando is not the kind of person who would allow her any kind of choice. He has decided to marry her, and that is what he is determined to do!"

"But why has she given him any encouragement at all?" He did not yet sound completely convinced.

"Look, Carlos, before you can hope to understand this, you must have some idea of what Julieta's circumstances were like in Johannesburg. Lonely, heartbroken, without her parents, and the only one in our office who was not free to go out with men, it comforted her to have a secret romance going on. Man, she's hardly more than a child! Don't you think that any young girl likes to have a young man make a fuss of her? Fernando had found out long ago that she was mentioned in her grandmother's will, and consequently his dedication was almost pitiful!"

"I see it all clearly. Yes!" he said, as if a light had suddenly gone up for him. "It is understandable that that could happen. But what are we going to do about it?"

I thought seriously about this for a few minutes. Then I said: "Carlos, you must stay and have dinner here with me tonight. Let us go back to the hotel now, and after supper I'll tell you the whole story. At the same time, if you are interested, I shall update my own."

"I suppose you know that there was a tremendous hullabaloo when Ricardo came home and heard that you were gone?" he asked me while we walked slowly back to the hotel. His expression had already brightened.

I looked at him incredulously. "But where was Ricardo? Wasn't he at the *palacio* while all this was going on?"

"Of course not!" Carlos looked at me as if he could hardly believe his ears. "Do you really think that he would have allowed Julieta to treat you like that if he had been there? I tell you, he nearly had a fit when he found out! He suddenly left, even before dinner that night, and I heard last night from Noël Estardos that he remained in Estoril for quite a few days after that. Noël says that he, Ricardo, left there in a foul mood!

"By the time I encountered you in the passage he must already have been in Estoril".

I took a deep breath and sent up a prayer of gratitude. One problem that had been weighing very heavily on my mind was slowly dissipating. I cannot bear to be misjudged or falsely accused, and it was a relief not to have to carry that burden around with me.

"I'm so glad to hear that, Carlos," I said. "It really hurt me to think that he could insult me like that."

He nodded sympathetically. "I can well believe it. When he came home again, our dear little Julieta—why do continue to waste my time on the girl?—was of course the first to bring him up to date."

"It seems that Ricardo was greatly upset by what she told him, but when he heard that you had gone, he was almost beside himself. Noël told me. ... He left immediately and wanted to go in search of you. Ricardo I mean—not Noel!"

"Why didn't he come and look for me here? He might have guessed that I would come to this place. After all, I don't know Lisbon very well."

"Yes, but evidently he thought that you were with Cameron Munroe. ... Remember, only I knew where you were, and I only came back on the scene again last night."

By this time we had reached the hotel. Carlos held the door open for me and he waited until I was inside before remarking: "Oh, by the way, Erin, I went to Monroe's hotel on Sunday evening, but he's not there, you know. I was told that he had left there on the same night!"

147

"What!" I cried, and stopped dead in my tracks. "What!" Wonderful, glorious relief began to flow through my entire being.—Then he had not purposely turned his back on me! The world was a wonderful place after all, and all the people around me were my friends!

"Oh, Carlos!" I whispered, overwhelmed, "How will we ever find out where he is now?"

"Fortunately I also learned that he had told the hotel manager that he would send a forwarding address as soon as he had decided where he was going to be. I thus left a relatively short note and requested that it be forwarded later when they had his address. He has quite a lot of contacts here, doesn't he?"

"Yes, but he could also be as far away as Germany. He traveled around a lot when he was last on the Continent."

Then another problem suddenly assailed me. "Did you think of telling him where to find *me* ?"

Carlos looked very apologetic. "Oh no! I'm sorry but I clean forgot. Now he is probably going to look for you at the *palacio*!"

After dinner we found a quiet corner on the balcony and I was then able to tell him the whole story of Fernando. I recounted it very carefully, ending in great detail with what he had said to me on the night of my party, upon hearing which Carlos sat bolt upright with indignation. "The lousy crook!" he exclaimed heatedly. "He actually had the gall to suggest that you and he become partners in the conspiracy?"

I nodded. "Obviously he had already decided that I was determined to derive as much as I possibly could from my friendship with Julieta and Ricardo!"

After that, and feeling somewhat guilty about it, I told of how I had accompanied Julieta when she went to meet Fernando in Sintra. About the night I went to meet him alone, how angry Ricardo was when he saw me there; and, finally, how Julia had swallowed everything that Fernando had fed her with reference to my 'betrayal' of her.

"The little fool! Carlos remarked bitterly. "I wish I could put her across my lap and give her a jolly good spanking. But you know, Erin,"—-immediately it was once more the protective lover speaking—"you really can't blame her. I know it's ridiculous, and you know that also, but a rogue as cunning as you say Fernando is, even managed to make a very strong case against you."

Fortunately I succeeded in not voicing aloud the sarcastic response with which I could so easily have responded, namely: *"Julieta can't have too much faith in her friends if he can so easily pit her against them!"* ... Instead I simply said: "Yes that's true and what are we going to do about it?"

Obviously Carlos had already decided, because he rose determinedly and straightened his tie. "When only you knew the truth, there was nothing for Fernando to fear, but now two of us know, and I'm a man—not a gentle, soft-hearted female. First I'm going to phone the *palacio* to get Fernando's address, then I am going straight to confront the villain. I intend to give him an opportunity to disappear quietly, or threaten to give him a good beating. After that I shall go to Ricardo and tell him everything!"

"And where does Julieta fit into this?" I asked with a teasing smile. "When should I go and choose the wedding present?"

"We'll have to wait for a suitable moment before I can hope to do a good imitation of Gregory Peck," he grinned. "Just give me a moonlit night, and then you'll see!"

He left there imbued with hope and in high spirits. As he later told me, he phoned someone (I can't remember who) from Lisbon station to get Fernando's address and then took a train to Sintra. From Sintra station he walked to Fernando's lodgings.

To his surprise it apparently did not take too much to scare Pereira. If I had only been there, I could have warned him about how certain animals play dead until the unsuspecting enemy is standing right over them. True to form, Fernando covered his face with his hands while, almost sobbing, he admitted that he had 'sinned'. He besought the other man to have mercy, after which Carlos left there filled with self-confidence. Next day he confessed that in that keyed up state he did not even need a taxi. Quickly and with a new spring in his step he easily walked the two miles to the *palacio*. Since then he has told me that he sang almost all the way.

When he turned in at the great wrought iron gates and began to walk up the winding path to the house, he was singing at the top of his voice. Hands in his pockets he looked around him to see if there wasn't perhaps a full moon and was not surprised to see one actually creeping out from behind the clouds!

It was while he stood there, carried away by his own thoughts, that he became aware for first time of a rustling in the bushes behind him. Before he could turn around, the attacker was upon him. Fernando brought the staff he carried, down hard, and then there was the sound of a dull thud before Carlos sagged under the blow—falling to his knees, but fortunately succeeding in jerking himself around sufficiently to catch Fernando about the legs They rolled around in the dust, one as murderous as the other, and fought so viciously that neither of them noticed the light of an approaching car.

Carlos dealt the other man blow for blow, for probably about two minutes; then, with a thrill of fear, he was made to realize that the blow Fernando had dealt him was now counting against him. Suddenly his legs gave way beneath him and, with a groan, he collapsed, and, Fernando, eagerly pouncing on top of him, immediately began to search his pockets

Cameron—who had retained the use of the hired car—of course had to stop when he saw the two writhing figures before him in the driveway. He jumped out without turning the lights off, and, as he rushed forward, he caught sight of a knife in the beam of light. His footsteps on the gravel startled Fernando, and the next moment he was running through the undergrowth with Cam in full speed behind him.

In an open place between the bushes, Cameron, benefiting from the stamina acquired through much regular exercise, easily caught up with him. He caught him by the collar of his shirt and roughly swung him around! "So it's you!" he exclaimed, and dealt Fernando a knockout blow on the chin. He was still lying there when Cam returned with Ricardo and Noël.

He helped Ricardo to carry Carlos inside, while Noël and Denis, the chauffeur, kept watch beside Fernando, and Carlos later maintained that the first voice he heard when he began to come round, was that of Cam asking: "Where is Erin?" ... He naturally expected to find me there, too.

Ricardo then had to admit that he was not sure. "Until Carlos left here this afternoon to go and visit her, I was under the impression that she was with you. Now I suspect that she must be in Lisbon, *Señhor*—at the hotel where she and Julieta originally stayed."

"You *suspect*, Ricardo!" Cameron repeated angrily, foregoing the more formal form of address. "How is it that you're not certain, man? In any case, what is she doing alone in Lisbon? What's been going on here?"

An uncomfortable silence followed. Ricardo apologetically cleared his throat and, finally avoiding the issue, suggested that Cameron should wait and ask Carlos.

"I think he knows where she is. Let us first summon the doctor to come and have a look at him, and then we can go and discuss this unhappy situation over a cognac in my study!"

Just then Julieta burst into the room, followed by a very distressed Inez.

"What's going on here?" she asked, precisely as Cameron had done a few moments before. The next minute she saw a pale and weak Carlos resting on the sofa—not a pleasant sight with his bloody face and torn, soiled clothing—and she immediately rushed forward to kneel on the floor beside him.

"How did you come to have such an accident?" she demanded frantically.

When the police made their appearance, she was still gently sponging his face. Inez stood by with a glass of brandy which she would periodically hold to his lips, and Carlos—who probably enjoyed the whole affair thoroughly, in spite of the hammering in his head—had the audacity to wink slyly at Cameron before, he, Cam, left the room with Ricardo.

Alone together in Ricardo's study the two men eyed one another suspiciously. What exactly they said to each other no one will ever know. Because both were refined gentleman they could not quarrel like common rapscallions, but one thing is certain: Cameron would surely have read Ricardo the riot act.

Perfect host that he was, Ricardo would perhaps have offered Cam a cigar (which he would politely have declined) and a drink of his choice (which he would have accepted) and then they would have discussed trivial matters, while constantly remaining conscious of the enmity between them, which could not be erased until they had candidly discussed the cause of it. After that—I sincerely hoped—they would be able to regain their mutual respect of days gone by.

Knowing Cameron as I did, after years of listening to him in court, he would certainly have been the first to introduce the subject, and bit by bit they would have unraveled the great misunderstanding. Later I heard that Ricardo had confessed that, before all this had come to pass, he had asked me to be his wife; and Cameron, in turn, had told him how, way back in Johannesburg, we had already feared that Fernando would cause trouble.

One mystery they could not elucidate was my secret visit to Fernando on that ill-fated Sunday night. They could only conclude that the telephone call I had received prior to that must have been from him, and that I had not gone of my own volition. Ricardo told me next day that Cameron was livid when appraised of the circumstances under which I had left there.

"It is absolutely disgraceful!" he cried indignantly "Nothing short of scandalous that you people could have insulted a woman like Erin in such a manner. It makes my blood boil when I consider how kind she has been to Julieta. Only think of what she had to give up to come with her to Portugal!"

Later, when Ricardo humbly admitted this to me, only I knew what he, Ricardo, could only suspect—how great the sacrifice was, and how powerful such love must be, for Cam to have risen and said, with a gesture of resignation: "Well,

Ricardo, it seems to me that you are indeed sufficiently contrite to appreciate her in future. I pray that you will make her happy and if you are certain that you can indeed do so, I wish you every happiness!

"It is too late to go to her hotel, of course, but if you will take my advice, you will be there on your knees very early tomorrow morning to beg her forgiveness! ... And now, if you will excuse me, I shall have to make tracks. It is a fair distance back to Lisbon and I am not absolutely sure that my room is still available to me!"

Chapter Twelve

Through my bedroom window I happened to see—with a measure of disbelief, because I had still not learned to regard it as a commonplace occurrence—the spectacular vehicle bearing the Monsaraz insignia, draw up downstairs in front of the hotel. I was thus unprepared, and it was consequently in a confused state of both pleased anticipation and nervousness that I went to meet Ricardo after the messenger had informed me that a visitor awaited me in the lounge next door. At that time on a Sunday morning that room was usually deserted.

Ricardo was standing at the window looking out across the city, but he swung around immediately when he heard me come in.

"Erin!" He came to meet me with outstretched hands, but uncertainly lowered them again as if he had suddenly been reminded of something. Although, unknown to me, his problems and doubts had already been dispelled on the previous night, he probably realized at that moment that it was not a foregone conclusion that I would feel the same. "Erin..." he repeated, uncertainly this time, and, waiting for me to be seated, he remained standing a small distance from me.

"For the first time since I became a man," he began, "I am today going to apologize to someone. Because it is not a habit with me, my apology may sound rather clumsy to you—but beloved, believe me when I say 'I am sorry!' ... I *am,* Erin. And if you wish it, I will willingly go on my knees to prove it!"

If I had really loved him, it would have been more difficult for me. I might have sat there, aloof and waiting for him to convince me. I would have made him suffer for a while so that the reunion would be sweeter and the making-up more passionate. As it was, the resolution was not quite so complicated for me. I smiled with un-assumed sadness and shook my head.

"No, Ricardo, that is not necessary. There is very little for which you need apologize, because I can easily picture how my actions must have appeared to you. I also behaved very unwisely and I realize now that I should have been honest with you sooner. I take it that Carlos has spoken to you?"

He nodded affirmatively. "He and Cameron Munroe, too."

"He has spoken to you? ... He came to talk to you? Where? ... When?"

"Last night at the *palacio*." And then he filled me in on what had occurred on the previous night.

"Poor Carlos!" I cried concernedly. "Is he any better today?" ... I had to fight the desire to find out more about Cam!

"Much better it seems. The doctor gave him a thorough examination last night and called again this morning. He is of the opinion that another day in bed will do wonders. Things are not going as well with his opponent, however. Your *Senhor* Monroe must have a fist of steel!"

"Cameron?" I inquired eagerly. "What did he have to do with all this?"

Ricardo smiled at the recollection. "I forgot to tell you about that. It was he who finally put our friend Fernando to sleep. He happened to come upon them just as the villain brought a knife to light, and I shudder to think what would have happened if Cameron had not appeared on the scene just in time."

"And Julieta?" I asked, with an effort at nonchalance. "How are things with her?"

"She was keen to come with me this morning—to ask for forgiveness, as she put it—but I persuaded her to stay home today. Besides; there is somebody else who is now occupying much of her time."

The first happy smile I had thus far seen on his countenance, now lit up his face and his eyes sparkled. "You do not know how deeply I hoped that your suspicions in that direction were not groundless, Erin. Now I intend to do everything in my power to help those two."

"That's wonderful!" I said with sincere joy. "They deserve to be happy."

"And we?" Ricardo asked unexpectedly, urgently, his face earnest once more . "Erin, *querida*, what of us?"

With a feeling of panic I realized that the moment I had dreaded had finally dawned. His last question had made it impossible to postpone the reckoning any longer and I shrank from the thought of what I had to do. More because it was necessary for me to move, than anything else, I jumped up and went to sit on a low sofa nearby me, from where I beckoned to him. "Please come and sit here beside me, Ricardo. I must talk to you."

His eagerness and the expectation on his face as he complied with my request, made my eyes swim. "When are you going to give me a response to the question I asked a week ago, Erin? The uncertainty is unbearable!"

I first drew a deep breath; then I took his hand in both of mine.

"Ricardo, I find the answer I must give you, very difficult to say, mainly because you will think I'm talking absolute nonsense; but if you would be so good as to listen and allow and me to finish, you may also realize that there is no other solution."

He nodded in agreement, without saying a word. ... I think he anticipated what was coming.

"Ricardo, last week in your study we talked about the power of mutual attraction, especially when two people are as constantly in one another's company as you and I have been. You described it as a 'burning passion' and asked me if I felt it, too. I did! ... Why should I deny it? I did."

"With me, as possibly in your case, it was more than mere mutual attraction. ... It was very close to love ... but is that enough? Is that enough to reassure you when your conscience plagues you? And you know very well that that is already the case. ... Is it enough to compensate me for my country and my people?—Think well before you answer.

"Now be that man who relies on common sense and always abides by a code that demands duty above all else, even his heart. ... *Dom* Gil and *Tia* Louisa, both people for whom you have a high regard, expect that you will someday be their son-in-law. ... Isabella—a wonderfully suitable person to be the next Marquise da Monsaraz—relies on you.

"In that lovely girl I see something of myself after the death of my parents. ... What, for want of a better word, I can only describe as 'lifelessness!' She is also like that as the result of bereavement.

"You are a very powerful man, Ricardo da Monsaraz—and I don't mean physically, socially, or financially. I'm referring to your personality. You have the ability to bring Isabella back to life. You can give her children, fulfill her and make her life seem worthwhile again. So, talking about *us*—is passion enough?"

We sat in silence for a long time. When I'd begun to wonder if he would ever respond, he unexpectedly asked: "Is it Cameron Munroe, *Pequena?*"

Because I thought too much of him to deceive him I could only nod affirmatively. I know that I also spoke the truth when I said, with an enormous lump in my throat: "I shall never forget you, Ricardo. A special place in my heart will forever belong to you. You have helped to make this month of April which I have spent in Portugal, unforgettable; because you see, a certain *Dom* Ricardo will always be remembered as the first man with whom I ever fell in love in my whole life!"

After he had left I remained for some time staring through the window with unseeing eyes. After that I paced back and forth undecidedly, until I was no longer unsure and knew exactly what I had to do. It was high time to set all pride aside. Cameron had already put up with enough from me and if I wanted him, I had to be the one to take the first step this time.

My heart beat tumultuously as I ran down the steps to the telephone. With trembling fingers I dialed the phone number and then held my breath while the hotel operator put me through to his room.

"Cameron?" I asked with some trepidation..

"Yes," he answered, sleepily at first and then suddenly sounded wide awake. "Is that you, Erin?"

"Yes," I said. "It's me. ... Oh Cameron I *must* see you! There is something that I very much want to discuss with you."

A long silence followed. "I don't know if I shall find time today," he said at last. "Is it so important? Has Ricardo been there?"

"Yes. He has just left. (*"Oh, Cam,"* I pleaded in my heart, *"Please don't say it's too late!"*) Please Cameron. I would very much like to come to you, but, as you have a car, it would be easier for you to come here. ... Please will you come?"

"Okay I'll come." —Even over the telephone I could hear that he said that reluctantly, and my courage almost deserted me.—"Don't I always come when you call me?"

A wonderful thought suddenly occurred to me. "Can't we go to Santa Clara again? There's no place here where one can talk. Just the park, and it's already crowded with prams[9], children and dogs!"

Another long silence while he considered this.

"Very well then," he agreed. "I still have to take a shower and have a shave, but I can probably be there in about half-an-hour.

During the half hour I had to wait, I got dressed and, believe me, no bride ever paid more attention to her appearance. One dress after another was hastily pulled out of the cupboard; then it was my hair that just would not look right. First my lipstick was too red for my liking, and then I could not decide what face powder to use. Was it too warm for perfume? Cameron will never guess how I prepared to enchant

---

9   baby carriages

him! If the poor man had only known it, the battle was over for him before it even began.

We drove in tense silence until we reached Santa Clara, with only a polite remark periodically to relieve the tension. Unfortunately it was too late to visit the little church again; the service had already been underway for quite some time. Consequently we passed it by and stopped again where we had parked the week before.

Nervous and yet simultaneously excited, I walked ahead of him and flung myself down on the grass beside the river. He followed more slowly. It was quite warm and above the rushing of the water the chanting of the many voices in the church was clearly carried to us on a gentle morning breeze.

"It is really delightful here," I remarked, chiefly to break the silence between us. "You know, Cam, I have been feeling bad all week because I didn't thank you for the pleasant time I spent here with you last Sunday."

He broke off a stalk of grass and began to chew it. "Is that what you wanted to see me about?" he asked wryly.

"Of course not" Clearly I could expect little encouragement from him! "I wanted to see you in order to apologize. In am so sorry for what I said to you. You made me very angry, and you know how it is. ... With sufficient provocation people sometimes say things they do not mean."

"Yes," he said, "I do know. I do indeed! You say that Ricardo came to see you this morning?"

"Yes, Very early...!"

"And does the world appear more rose-colored now?"

"It does, A lot more!"

Cam looked up and with an obvious effort said: "So he asked you to marry him?"

"Yes, he did, but he had already done so last Sunday. I was to give him my answer this morning, and fortunately you had already helped me that day to decide what my answer would be today."

He made no comment, so I carried on ....

"Cameron, I received a letter from Angela yesterday. ... She maintains that one should never marry until you find that one person in a million who is the right one for you. That's what I wanted to talk to you about...."

"And you have found him now?"

"I have!"

He sat bolt upright and grasped me by my shoulders. "No! No!" He called out passionately. ... "No, no Erin! Do not tell me! Why do you so enjoy torturing me? How have you suddenly become such a sadist? Do you like to see me caught like an insect on a pin so that you can watch me squirm?"

With inner satisfaction I decided to disregard this outburst. I got up and went to stand some distance away from him.

"I'm going home shortly, Cameron."

"Don't you like Portugal anymore, or are you planning to come back?"

"Yes, most certainly I am. I like it here, and I hope to come back someday, but I'm first going home to prove something to you."

Obviously he had not expected this. An expression of bewilderment crossed his face. "To prove something to *me*? And what might that be?"

It wasn't easy to tell him. ... I felt a warm flush begin to creep up my neck and could only stammer, "I want to prove to you—no wait, how did you put it? ... I want to *prove* to you that I can be a far better lawyer's wife than I ever was a secretary...!"

Before I could complete the sentence, he had already begun to rise to his feet, and I rejoiced to watch the doubt disappear from his face to give way to an expression of incredulous wonderment.

"Don't you understand, you dear, precious fool," I said with a thrill in my voice, and stretched out my arms to him. "What I'm trying to say is that I love you! ... I love you, Cameron Monroe!"

He had kissed me once before—but not like this. In his fierce embrace I closed my eyes, overcome by the ecstasy that flowed through me when his lips found mine. Urgently, fiercely at first, his kiss eventually became gentle and very tender.

"Erin! My own sweetheart! My own little girl!"

Little by little my arms had crept round his neck. I had to stand on my toes so that I could only draw him closer in case he tried to escape. "Cameron, my darling," I whispered after a while, and smiled through the tears that dimmed my eyes. "If I'd known that it would be like this, I would never have waited so long to kiss you!"

He laughed jubilantly, his teeth sparkling white in the tan of his face. His arms tightened convulsively around me. "Did I not try to convince you long ago that I am the one you love?"

I raised my face to be kissed again.

Behind us, in the distance, we could hear the bells of Santa Clara...

April in Portugal

Writer meets one of her characters

A story behind a story...

TRANSLATION from the Kempton News 1956

This can indeed happen—but then only in books she has written. She can contrive all manner of situations and have her characters turn up in the most impossible places, and readers will delight in them, ascribing all the wonder and the magic to the chief character while not caring one bit about how she casts her magic spells.

When Mrs. Marie Warder of Aston Manor recently met one of the main characters in her book, *April in Portugal,* face-to-face, she first have thought that she was a victim of her own imagination (of which she must surely possess a good deal if one takes into consideration the fact that she has already published 16 novels) was playing tricks on her, for things like this did not occur in real life. And yet, here stood the woman right in front of her!

About 18 years ago Mrs. Warder explains, she made the acquaintance of a young Portuguese girl, Julieta Machado da Cruz of Lourenco Marques. "Julieta was on the point of getting married and while she was in South Africa to buy her trousseau, I was asked to keep an eye on her and to assist with her shopping. She and I talked a great deal, and what she told me about herself formed the background to one of my books which followed soon after that."

The book appeared, Julieta was married, and as far as Mrs. Warder was concerned, the pleasant episode belonged to the past. It usually happens that one meets someone, gets to know him or her, and then never see them again. One's paths go in different directions—and each has their own interests.

"Recently Julieta turned up at my home and how she found me, would, I thought, make a good plot for yet another story. In one word it is 'fantastic and very rare that anything like this can really happen. "

It turns out that Julieta's daughter was sent to a convent in Witbank to completely her schooling. There she learned to read, write and speak Afrikaans fluently.

One day she was browsing in the school library and came across a book called 'April in Portugal.' Since she was of Portuguese descent the title of the book naturally attracted her attention, immediately.

She took it out of the library and, on the very first page, she saw a name that was very familiar to her—her mother's maiden name!

The girl was ecstatic. She took the novel along with her on the very first opportunity she had to visit her parents, and told them the whole exciting story. The mother, Julieta, could well remember her visit to South Africa, and the friendly South African who had so kindly helped her at that time.

The family then went to great lengths to find Mrs. Warder, and there. on the dust cover of the book, they found in the answer. A short biography in which it was stated that Marie Warder was married to a Mr. Tom Warder, attached to South African Airways in Kempton Park, and they then lost no time in deciding to come to Kempton Park, where they made inquiries at the airline's head office, found the Warders, and this is how the exciting reunion took place after 18 years!

Made in the USA
Charleston, SC
17 June 2011